Born in Jerusalem in 1939, Amos Oz is one of Israel's finest living writers and also well known as a political commentator and campaigner for peace in the Middle East. He is the author of many previous books of fiction, including *The Same Sea, My Michael, Black Box, To Know A Woman, Fima* and *Don't Call It Night,* as well as acclaimed works of non-fiction, *In the Land of Israel, The Slopes of Lebanon, Israel, Palestine & Peace* and *The Story Begins.* His work has been translated into twenty-eight languages and he as won many international literary awards. Amos Oz is married, with two daughters and a son, and lives in Arad, Israel.

Nicholas de Lange, the translator, teaches at the University of Cambridge and writes on a variety of subjects. He has won prizes for his translations, and has translated nine books by Amos Oz.

WITHDRAWN FROM STOCK

ALSO BY AMOS OZ

Fiction

My Michael
Elsewhere, Perhaps
Touch the Water, Touch the Wind
Unto Death
The Hill of Evil Counsel
Where the Jackals Howl
A Perfect Peace
Black Box
To Know A Woman
Fima
Don't Call It Night
The Same Sea

Non-Fiction

In the Land of Israel
The Slopes of Lebanon
Under This Blazing Light
Israel, Palestine & Peace
The Story Begins

For Children

Soumchi

Amos Oz

PANTHER IN THE BASEMENT

TRANSLATED FROM THE HEBREW BY
Nicholas de Lange

J40729

WITHDRAWN FROM STOCK

LIMERICK COUNTY LIBRARY

WITHDRAWN FROM STOCK

VINTAGE

Published by Vintage 1997

4 6 8 10 9 7 5

Copyright © Amos Oz 1995

English translation copyright © Nicholas de Lange 1997

The right of Amos Oz to be identified as the author of this work has
been asserted by him in accordance with the Copyright, Designs and
Patents Act, 1988

The right of Nocholas de Lange to be identified as the translator of
this work has been asserted by him in accordance with the Copyright,
Designs and Patents Act, 1988

This book is sold subject to the condition that it shall not, by way of
trade or otherwise be lent, resold, hired out, or otherwise circulated
without the publisher's prior consent in any form of binding or cover
other than that in which it is published and without a similar
condition including this condition being imposed on the subsequent
purchaser

First published in Hebrew as *Panter Bamartef* by
Keter Publishing House, Jerusalem, 1995

First published in Great Britain by
Vintage 1997

Vintage
Random House, 20 Vauxhall Bridge Road, London SW1V 2SA

Random House Australia (Pty) Limited
20 Alfred Street, Milsons Point, Sydney,
New South Wales 2061, Australia

Random House New Zealand Limited
18 Poland Road, Glenfield,
Auckland 10, New Zealand

Random House (Pty) Limited
Endulini, 5A Jubilee Road, Parktown 2193, South Africa

The Random House Group Limited Reg. No. 954009

www.randomhouse.co.uk

A CIP catalogue record for this Book
is available from the British Library

ISBN 0099754010

Papers used by Random House are natural, recyclable products made
from wood grown in sustainable forests. The manufacturing processes
conform to the environmental regulations of the country of origin

Set in 10½/12 Sabon by SX Composing DTP, Rayleigh, Essex

Printed and bound in Great Britain by
Bookcraft Bath

For Dean, Nadav and Alon

WITHDRAWN FROM STOCK

WITHDRAWN FROM STOCK

Editorial Note

The films mentioned in the text are fictional. Their titles, plots and casts were invented by the author to conjure up the popular Hollywood films which were showing in Jerusalem in the late 1940s, and which he himself watched there as a child in the local cinema.

WITHDRAWN FROM STOCK

I

I HAVE BEEN CALLED a traitor many times in my life. The first time was when I was twelve and a quarter and I lived in a neighbourhood at the edge of Jerusalem. It was during the summer holidays, less than a year before the British left the country and the State of Israel was born out of the midst of war.

One morning these words appeared on the wall of our house, painted in thick black letters, just under the kitchen window: PROFI BOGED SHAFEL 'Proffy is a low-down traitor.' The word *shafel*, 'low-down', raised a question that still interests me now, as I sit and write this story. Is it possible for a traitor not to be low-down? If not, why did Chita Reznik (I recognized his writing) bother to add the word 'low-down'? And if it is, under what circumstances is treachery not low-down?

I had had the nickname Proffy ever since I was so high. It was short for Professor, which they called me because of my obsession with checking words. (I still love words: I like collecting, arranging, shuffling, reversing, combining them. Rather the way people who love money do with coins and banknotes and people who love cards do with cards.)

My father saw the writing under the kitchen window when he went out to get the newspaper at half past six that morning. Over breakfast, while he was spreading raspberry jam on a slice of black bread, he suddenly plunged the knife into the jam jar almost up to the handle and said in his deliberate way:

'What a pleasant surprise. And what has His Lordship been

1

up to now, that we should deserve this honour?'

My mother said:

'Don't get at him first thing in the morning. It's bad enough that he's always being got at by other children.'

Father was dressed in khaki, like most men in our neighbourhood in those days. He had the gestures and voice of a man who is definitely in the right. Dredging up a sticky mass of raspberry from the bottom of the jar and spreading an equal amount on both halves of his slice of bread, he said:

'The fact is that almost everyone nowadays uses the word "traitor" too freely. But what is a traitor? Yes indeed. A man without honour. A man who secretly, behind your back, for the sake of some questionable advantage, helps the enemy to work against his people. Or to harm his family and friends. He is more despicable than a murderer. Finish your egg, please. I read in the paper that people are dying of hunger in Asia.'

My mother pulled my plate towards her and finished my egg and the rest of my bread and jam, not because she was hungry but for the sake of peace. She said:

'Anyone who loves isn't a traitor.'

My mother addressed these words neither to me nor to Father: to judge by the direction she was looking, she was talking to a nail that was stuck in our kitchen wall just above the icebox and served no particular purpose.

WITHDRAWN FROM STOCK

2

AFTER BREAKFAST MY parents hurried off to catch their bus to work. I was free, with oceans of time ahead of me till the evening, because it was the summer holidays. First of all I cleared the table and put everything away in its proper place, in the icebox, the cupboards, or the sink, because I loved being at home on my own all day without anything to do. I washed the dishes and left them upside down to drain dry. Then I went round the apartment closing the windows and shutters, so as to have a shady den till evening. The sun and the dust from the desert were liable to damage my father's books that lined the walls, some of which were rare volumes. I read the morning paper, then I folded it and put it on the kitchen table, and I put my mother's brooch away in its case. I did all this not like a repentant low-down traitor but from love of tidiness. To this day I make a habit of going round the house every morning and evening putting everything in its right place. Five minutes ago, as I was writing about closing the windows and shutters, I stopped writing because I remembered to get up and close the bathroom door; though it might have preferred to stay open, to judge by the groan it made as I closed it.

All that summer my mother and father went out at eight o'clock in the morning and came home at six in the evening. My lunch was waiting for me in the icebox and my days were clear as far as the horizon. For instance, I could start the game with a small group of five or ten soldiers on the rug, or pioneers, surveyors, road makers, and fort builders, and step by step we could tame the forces of nature, defeat enemies, conquer wide-open spaces, build towns and villages, and lay out roads connecting them.

My father was a proofreader and sort of editorial assistant in a small publishing house. At night he used to sit up till two or three o'clock in the morning, surrounded by the shadows of his bookshelves, with his body immersed in darkness and only his grey head floating in a ring of light from his desk lamp, as though he was laboriously climbing the gulley between the mountains of books piled up on his desk, filling slips and cards with notes in preparation for his great book on the history of the Jews in Poland. He was a principled, intense man, who was deeply committed to the concept of justice.

My mother, on the other hand, liked to raise her half-empty glass of tea and stare through it at the blue light in the window. And sometimes she would press it to her cheek, as though drawing warmth from the contact. She was a teacher in an institution for immigrant orphans who had managed to hide from the Nazis in monasteries or remote villages and had now reached us, as my mother said, 'straight from the darkness of the valley of the shadow of death'. At once she would correct herself: 'They come from a place where men behave like wolves to each other. Even refugees. Even children.' In my mind I would associate the remote villages with horrifying images of wolf-men and the darkness of the valley of the shadow of death. I loved the words 'darkness' and 'valley' because they immediately conjured up a valley shrouded in darkness, with monasteries and cellars. And I loved the shadow of death because I didn't understand it. If I whispered 'shadow of death', I could almost hear a kind of deep sound like the note that comes from the lowest key on the piano, a sound that draws after it a trail of dim echoes, as though a disaster has happened and now there is no going back.

I returned to the kitchen. I had read in the paper that we were living in a fateful period and therefore we must engage all our moral resources. And it also said that the actions of the British were 'casting a heavy shadow' and that the Hebrew nation was called upon to 'withstand the test'.

I left the house, looking all around me like in the resistance, to make sure no one was watching me: a strange man in sunglasses, for instance, who might be concealed behind a newspaper, lurking in the doorway of one of the buildings on the other side of the road. But the street seemed absorbed in its own preoccupations. The greengrocer was building a wall of empty crates. The boy who worked at the Sinopsky Brothers grocery was dragging a squeaking handcart. Childless old Pani Ostrowska was sweeping away at the pavement in front of her door, probably for the third time that morning. Doctor Gryphius was sitting on her balcony filling out filing cards: she was a spinster, and Father was helping her to gather material for her memoirs of Jewish life in her native town, Rosenheim, in Bavaria. And the paraffin seller went by slowly in his cart, the reins lying slack on his knees, ringing a handbell and singing a plaintive Yiddish song to his horse. So I stood there and scrutinized intently the black words PROFI BOGED SHAFEL, 'Proffy is a low-down traitor', in case there was some tiny detail that could shed a new light. From haste or fear the last letter of the word BOGED, 'traitor', had turned out more like an R than a D, making me not a low-down traitor, BOGED, but a low-down adult, BOGER. That morning I would gladly have given everything I had to be an adult.

So Chita Reznik had 'done a Balaam'.

Mr Zerubbabel Gihon, our Bible and Judaism teacher, had explained to us in class:

'Doing a Balaam. When a curse comes out as a blessing. For instance, like when the British minister Ernest Bevin said in Parliament in London that the Jews are a stubborn race, he did a Balaam.'

Mr Gihon had a habit of seasoning his lessons with witticisms that were not funny. He often used his wife as the butt of his jokes. For instance, when he wanted to illustrate the passage from the Book of Kings about whips and scorpions, he said: 'Scorpions are a hundred times worse than whips. I afflict you with whips and my wife afflicts me with scorpions.' Or: 'There is a text that says, "As the crackling of thorns under a pot". Ecclesiastes, chapter seven. Like Mrs Gihon trying to sing.'

Once I said during supper:

'You know my teacher Gihon, hardly a day goes by when he isn't unfaithful to his wife in class.'

My father looked at my mother and said:

'Your son has definitely taken leave of his senses.' (My father was fond of the word 'definitely'. And also of the words 'indubitably', 'evidently', 'yes indeed'.)

My mother said:

'Instead of insulting him, why don't you try to find out what he's trying to say? You never really listen to him. Or to me. Or to anybody. All you ever listen to is the news on the wireless.'

'Everything in the world,' Father replied calmly, refusing as usual to be drawn into an argument, 'has at least two sides. As is well known to all but a few frenetic souls.'

I didn't know what 'frenetic souls' meant, but I did know that this was not the right moment to ask. So I let them sit facing each other in silence for nearly a full minute – they sometimes had silences that resembled arm-wrestling – and only then did I say:

'Except a shadow.'

My father shot me one of his suspicious glances, with his glasses halfway down his nose, nodding his head up and down, one of those looks that conjure up what we learned in Bible class, 'he looked that it should bring forth grapes, and it brought forth wild grapes', and his blue eyes above his glasses shone at me in naked disappointment, with me and with young people in general and with the failure of the educational system that had been entrusted with a butterfly and had sent back a chrysalis:

'What do you mean "shadow". It's your brain that's the shadow.'

My mother said:

'Instead of silencing him, why don't you find out what he's trying to say? He must be trying to say something.'

And Father:

'Right. Yes indeed. Well then, what is Your Lordship getting at this evening? What mysterious shadow are you deigning to report to us about this time? "Thou seest the shadow of mountains as if they were men"? "As a servant desireth the

6

shadow"?'

I got up to go to bed. I didn't owe him any explanation. Nevertheless, beyond the call of duty, I said:

'Except a shadow, Dad. You said a moment ago that everything in the world has at least two sides. And you were almost right. But you were forgetting that a shadow, for instance, only has one side. Go and check, if you don't believe me. You could even do an experiment or two. Didn't you yourself teach me that it's the exception that proves the rule and that one shouldn't generalize. You've forgotten what you taught me.'

So saying, I got up and cleared the table, then went to my room.

3

SITTING IN MY father's chair at his desk, I took down the big dictionary and the encyclopedia, and, just as I had learned to do from him, I started to compile a list of words on a blank piece of card.

Traitor: turncoat, defector, deserter, renegade, informer, sneak, collaborator, stool-pigeon, saboteur, spy, fifth-columnist, plant, mole, foreign agent, double agent, *agent provocateur*, Brutus (*see* Rome), Quisling (*see* Norway), Judas (*Christian usage*). *Adj.*: treacherous, disloyal, faith-less, unfaithful, perfidious, two-faced. *Vb.*: betray, deceive, break faith, deal treacherously, defect, play false, rat. *Phr.*: snake in the grass, wolf in sheep's clothing, stab in the back, do the dirty. *Bibl.*: Confidence in an unfaithful man in time of trouble is like a broken tooth (Prov. 25:19); they be all adulterers, an assembly of treacherous men (Jer. 9:2); wherefore lookest thou upon them that deal treacherously? (Hab. 1:13).

I closed the dictionary. I felt dizzy. This list appeared to me like a thick forest with many bifurcating paths from which more and more tracks spread out, losing themselves in the thickets, winding tortuously, joining up for a while and diverging again, leading to hideaways, containing caverns, undergrowth, labyrinths, cells, crannies, forsaken valleys, wonder and amazement. What connection is there between defect and desert, informer and adulterer, faithless and two-faced, saboteur and stabber, mole and rat? What dark deeds did Brutus and Quisling commit? And more: tracks and treks; tortuous and tortoise. (To this day I dare not open an encyclopedia or a dictionary when I am working. If I do, that's half a day lost.) I no longer cared what I was, a traitor, an argumentative child, a crazy child, all that morning I sailed on the wide seas of the encyclopedia, reaching savage war-painted tribes in Papua, strange craters on the surface of stars blazing with volcanic hellfire or the opposite, frozen and wreathed in eternal darkness (is that where the shadow of death lurks?), landing on islands, wandering lost through primeval swamps, encountering cannibals and hermits, godforsaken black-skinned Jews from the days of the Queen of Sheba, and I read about the continents drifting away from each other at a rate of half a millimetre a year. (How long could they go on drifting apart? Surely in billions of years' time, because the earth is spherical, they would meet up again on the other side!) Then I looked up Brutus and Quisling and I was going to look for Judas, too, but on the way I stopped at light-years and they overwhelmed me with piercing pleasure.

At midday hunger drove me from the origins of the universe to the kitchen. I bolted down the food my mother had left for me in the icebox: grits, a meatball, soup, don't forget to heat it all up for a few minutes on the stove and remember to turn it off afterwards. But I didn't heat it up: I couldn't spare the time. I was in a hurry to finish and get back to the vanishing galaxies. Suddenly I noticed under the door a folded note in Ben Hur's handwriting: 'To the low-down traitor take note. This evening at half past six present yourself without delay at the place you know in Tel Arza to face a Court Marshal for serious treachery namely frattenizing with the British persecutor. Signed: FOD Organization, High Command, Department of Internal Security and Interrogation. NB: bring sweater, water canteen and proper shoes because the questioning may last all night.'

First of all I corrected with a pencil: 'fraternizing' not 'frattenizing'; 'Martial' not 'Marshal'. Then I committed the message to memory in accordance with standing orders and burned the note in the kitchen, and I flushed the ashes down the toilet so as not to leave any clues, in case the British mounted a house-to-house search. Then I returned to the desk and tried to get back to the galaxies and light-years. But the galaxies had dispersed and the light-years had faded out. So I took another blank card from my father's little pile and noted: *The situation is serious and gives rise to anxiety*. And I wrote: *But our heads we'll hold up high*. Then I tore up the card and put the dictionary and the encyclopedia away. There was fear.

Which I must overcome at once.

But how?

I decided to look at some stamps. Barbados and New Caledonia were each represented in my collection by a single stamp. I managed to locate both places in the big German atlas. I looked for some chocolate but there wasn't any. In the end I went back to the kitchen and licked two spoonfuls of Father's raspberry jam.

Nothing helped. This was bad.

4

THIS IS HOW I remember Jerusalem in that last summer of British rule. A stone city sprawling over hilly slopes. Not so much a city as isolated neighbourhoods separated by fields of thistles and rocks. British armoured cars sometimes stood at street corners with their slits almost closed, like eyes dazzled by the light. And their machine guns sticking out in front like pointing fingers: You there!

At dawn the boys would go round sticking posters from the Underground on walls and lampposts. On Saturday afternoons, in our backyard, there were arguments with guests and a procession of glasses of scalding tea, and biscuits that my mother made (I would help her by printing star and flower shapes on the soft dough). In the course of these arguments both the guests and my parents would use words like persecution, extermination, salvation, intelligence, heritage, clandestine immigration, siege, demonstrations, Haj Amin, extremists, kibbutzim, the White Paper, the Hagganah, self-restraint, settlements, gangs, the conscience of the world, riots, protests, clandestine immigrants. Occasionally one of the guests would get carried away, often it would be one of the quiet ones, a skinny, pale-faced man with a cigarette trembling between his fingers and a shirt buttoned up to the neck, whose pockets were stuffed with notebooks and slips of paper, and he would explode with polite anger and shout expressions such as 'like sheep to the slaughter', 'Protected Jews', and then he would hurriedly add, as though in an attempt to correct the bad impression, 'But we must on no account allow ourselves to be split, heaven forbid, we're all in the same boat.'

The empty laundry room on the roof was fitted up with a washbasin and electric light, and Mr Lazarus, a tailor from Berlin, moved in. He was a small man, who blinked and nodded and, despite the heat of the summer, he was always dressed in a shabby grey jacket and a waistcoat. And he always carried a green tape-measure round his neck, like a necklace. His wife and daughters, people said, had been murdered by Hitler. How had Mr Lazarus himself managed to survive? There were various rumours. Uncertainties. I had my doubts: What did *they* know? After all, Mr Lazarus himself never said a word about what had happened. He put up a card in the entrance hall, half in German that I could not understand and half in Hebrew that he asked my mother to write for him: 'Expert tailor and cutter from Berlin. Commissions of all sorts undertaken. Alterations to order. Latest fashions. Reasonable prices. Credit available.' After a day or two somebody tore off the German half: we would not tolerate the language of the murderers here.

My father found an old woollen cardigan at the back of the wardrobe and sent me up to the roof to ask Mr Lazarus to be good enough to change the buttons and strengthen the seams. 'Yes indeed, it's only an old rag, possibly unwearable,' Father said, 'but he seems to be hungry for bread up there, and charity is offensive. So let's send it up to him. He can change the buttons. Earn a few piasters. Make him feel he's appreciated.'

My mother said:

'All right. New buttons. But why send the boy? Go yourself, talk to him, ask him in for a glass of tea.'

'Definitely,' said Father, sheepishly, and a moment later he added decisively: 'Yes indeed. We must definitely invite him.'

Mr Lazarus fenced in the far corner of the roof with old bedsteads, reinforced with wire, and made a kind of coop or cage, spread out some straw from an old mattress, bought half a dozen hens, and asked Mother to add in Hebrew on the remaining half of his notice: 'And fresh eggs for sale.' But he would never sell one of his hens to be killed and eaten, even for a feastday. On the contrary, they said Mr Lazarus had given

12

each hen a name, and that he used to go out on to the roof at night to check that they were sleeping soundly. One day Chita Reznik and I hid among the water tanks and heard Mr Lazarus arguing with his hens. In German. Declaring, insisting, explaining, even humming them a tune. Sometimes I took up some dry bread crumbs or a jar of reject lentils that my mother told me to pick out. When I was feeding the hens, Mr Lazarus would sometimes come and touch me suddenly on the shoulder with his fingertips, then he would shake his fingers as though he had burned himself. We had lots of people who talked to thin air. Or to someone who wasn't there.

On the roof, behind Mr Lazarus's chicken run, I installed a lookout post from which I had an excellent view of the other roofs; I could even squint into the British army camp. I used to stand there, concealed among the water tanks, spying on their evening roll call, noting down particulars in a notebook, and then I aimed a sniper's rifle at them and wiped them all out with a single economical, precise salvo.

From my lookout post on the roof I also had a view of far-away Arab villages scattered on the slopes of the hills, and the Mount of Olives and Mount Scopus, beyond the tops of which the desert abruptly began, while far away to the south-east lurked the Hill of Evil Counsel, on which stood Government House, the British High Commissioner's residence. I was working that summer on the last details of a plan to take it by storm, from three directions at once; I had even prepared a summary of the things I would say without any hesitation to the High Commissioner once he was caught and was being interrogated in my lookout post here on the roof.

Once, I was up on the roof inspecting Ben Hur's window because I suspected he was being followed, when, instead of Ben Hur, his older sister Yardena appeared in the window. She stood in the middle of the room and spun round a couple of times on tiptoe, like a dancer, and suddenly unbuttoning her housecoat she took it off and put on a dress. Between the housecoat and the dress, some dark patches stood out against her white skin, a couple under her arms and another dizzying island of shadow under her belly, but they were covered up at once by her dress, which fell like a curtain from her neck to her knees before I had time to see what I had seen or to retreat from my lookout or even to close my eyes. I really would have closed them, only it was all over in an instant. In that instant I thought: Now I'm going to die. I deserve to die for this.

Yardena had a fiancé and an ex-fiancé and it was said there was also a hunter from Galilee and a poet from Mount Scopus, as well as a shy admirer who only looked at her sadly and never had the courage to say anything more to her than 'Good morning' and 'What a nice day'. In the winter I had shown her a couple of my poems and after a few days she had said, 'You'll always write.' These words were more wonderful to me than most of the words I have heard in the course of the years, because I really do write.

That evening I made up my mind to speak to her boldly or at least to write to her boldly and apologize and explain that I hadn't meant to watch her and that I hadn't really seen anything. But I didn't do it, because I didn't know whether she had noticed me standing on the roof. Maybe she hadn't spotted me? I prayed she hadn't and yet I hoped she had.

I knew by heart all the neighbourhoods, villages, hills, and towers that were visible from my lookout post. In the Sinopsky Brothers grocery, in the queue at the clinic, on the Dorzions' balcony opposite, in front of the Shibboleth newsstand, people would stand and argue about the borders of the future Hebrew State. Would they include Jerusalem? Would they include the British naval base at Haifa? And what about Galilee? And the desert? Some hoped that the forces of the civilized world would come and protect us from being murdered by bloodthirsty Arabs. (Every nation had a fixed epithet, like a first name with a surname: perfidious Albion, tainted Germany, faraway China, Soviet Russia, rich America. Down on the coast there was bustling Tel Aviv. Far away from us, in Galilee, in the valleys, was the labouring Land of Israel. The Arabs were labelled bloodthirsty. Even the world had several epithets, depending on the atmosphere and the situation: civilized, free, wide, hypocritical. Sometimes people said: 'The world that knew and said nothing.' Sometimes they said: 'The world will not stay silent about this.')

In the meantime, until the British pulled out and the

14

Hebrew State finally emerged, the grocer's and the greengrocer's opened at seven in the morning and closed at six in the evening in time for the curfew. The neighbours – the Dorzions, Dr Gryphius, ourselves, Ben Hur and his parents – gathered at Dr Buster's because he had a radio. We listened in gloomy silence to the news on the Voice of Jerusalem. Sometimes, after dark, very softly, we listened to the clandestine broadcast of the Voice of Fighting Zion. Sometimes we stayed on after the news to listen to the appeals for missing relatives, in case they suddenly mentioned a relative murdered in Europe who turned out to have survived after all and had managed to make his way to the Land of Israel or at least to one of the DP camps that the British had set up in Cyprus.

There was silence in the room during the broadcast, like a curtain stirring in the breeze in the dark. But as soon as the radio was turned off everyone started talking. They talked incessantly. What had happened, what was going to happen, what might or could or should be done, what chances we had left: they talked as though they were afraid that something terrible would happen if a moment's silence should suddenly fall. If ever that cold grey silence peered over the shoulder of the discussion and argument, they silenced it immediately.

Everybody read the papers, and when they finished reading them they swapped with each other: *Davar*, *Hamashkif*, *Hatsofeh* and *Haarets* passed from hand to hand. And because the days were much longer then than they are nowadays, and each paper had only four pages, in the evening they reread what they had already scoured in the morning. They stood in a little group on the pavement in front of the Sinopsky Brothers grocery and compared what was written in *Davar* about our moral strength with what *Haarets* said concerning the importance of patience: was there possibly something crucial lurking between the lines that had been missed on the first and second reading?

Besides Mr Lazarus, there were other refugees in the neighbourhood, from Poland, Romania, Germany, Hungary, Russia. Most of the residents were not called 'refugees', nor were they termed 'pioneers' or 'citizens': they were described as 'the organized community', which was located more or less in the middle, beneath the pioneers and above the refugees, in opposition to the British and the Arabs but also opposed to the militants. But how could you tell the difference? Almost all of them, pioneers and refugees and militants, spoke with throaty *r*s and liquid *l*s, except for the orientals who spoke with trilled *r*s and harsh guttural sounds. The parents hoped that we children would grow up to be a new kind of Jew, improved, broad-shouldered, fighters and tillers of the soil, which was why they stuffed us full of liver, chicken and fruit, so that when the time came we would stand up, bold and suntanned, and not let the enemy lead us like sheep to the slaughter again. Sometimes they would feel nostalgic for the places they had come here from: they would sing songs in languages we didn't know, and they would give us rough translations, so that we, too, would know that once upon a time there had been rivers and meadows, forests and fields, thatched roofs and bells ringing in the mist. Because here in Jerusalem the waste plots stood parched in the summer sun and the buildings were made of stone and corrugated iron, and the sun scorched everything as though war was here already. The dazzling light preyed on itself from morn to evening.

Occasionally someone would say: 'What's going to happen?', and somebody else would answer: 'We must hope for the best', or 'We've just got to carry on'. My mother would sometimes sit bent over a box of photos and mementos for five or ten minutes, and I knew that I had to pretend not to see. Her parents and her sister Tanya had been murdered by Hitler in the Ukraine, along with all the Jews who had not managed to get here in time. Father once said:

'It's incomprehensible. Simply unbelievable. And the whole world said nothing.'

He, too, grieved sometimes for his parents and his sisters, but not with tears: he would stand for half an hour or so, in the rather sour, angular pose of a man who is stubbornly in the right, and peer closely at the maps that were pinned up on the wall in the passage. Like a general in his HQ: staring and saying nothing. His view was that we must drive out the British occupier and set up a Hebrew State here that all persecuted Jews all over the world could come to. He said, 'It must evidently set a model of justice to the world, even towards the Arabs if they choose to stay and live here amongst us. Yes, despite everything the Arabs are doing to us, because of the people who are inciting them and egging them on, we will treat them with exemplary generosity, but definitely not out of weakness. When the free Hebrew State is finally established, no villain in the world will ever again dare to murder or humiliate Jews. If he does, we will smite him because when the time comes we will have a very long arm indeed.'

When I was in the fourth or fifth year at school I carefully traced the map of the world from Father's atlas in pencil on tracing paper, and I marked the promised Hebrew State: a green patch between the desert and the sea. From this green patch I drew a long arm across continents and seas, and at the end of the arm I put a fist that could reach everywhere. Even to Alaska. Beyond New Zealand.

'But what have we done,' I once asked over supper, 'to make everyone hate us so?'

My mother said:

'It's because we have always been in the right. They can't forgive us that we've never hurt a fly.'

I thought, though I didn't say it: It follows that it is definitely not worth being in the right.

And also: It explains Ben Hur's attitude. I am in the right, and I don't hurt a fly either. But from now on a new age will start: the age of the panther.

Father said:

'It is a sad and obscure question. In Poland, for example, they hated us because we were different, because we were strange, because we talked and dressed and ate differently from those around us. But a few miles away, across the border in Germany, they hated us for the opposite reason: in Germany we talked and ate and dressed and behaved exactly like everybody else. So the anti-semites said: "Look at them insinuating themselves, yes indeed, you can no longer tell who is a Jew and who isn't." That is our fate: the excuses for hatred change but the hatred itself continues forever. And what is the conclusion?'

'That we should try not to hate,' said my mother.

17

But Father, whose blue eyes blinked rapidly behind his glasses, said: 'We must not be weak. To be weak is a sin.'

'But what have we done?' I asked. 'How have we made them so angry?'

'That question,' Father said, 'you should put to our persecutors, not to us. And now would Your Lordship please pick up your sandals from under the chair and put them where they belong. No, not there. Not there either. Where they belong.'

At night we could hear shots and explosions in the distance: the Underground was coming out of its secret bases and attacking the centres of British government. By seven o'clock we would have closed the doors and shutters and shut ourselves in till the morning. There was a night curfew in the city. A clear breeze blew in the abandoned streets, along the alleys and up the winding stone steps. Sometimes we would start at the sound of a dustbin lid knocked off by an alley cat in the dark. Jerusalem stood still and waited. Inside our apartment there was silence most of the evening. Father sat with his back to us, separated from us in the ring of light cast by his desk lamp, dug in among his books and index cards, his fountain pen scratching at the silence, stopping, hesitating, then scratching again, as though it was digging a tunnel. Father was checking, comparing, perhaps pinning down a stray detail in the notes he was gathering for his great book on the history of the Jews in Poland. My mother would sit on the other side of the room, in her rocking chair, reading or, with her open book face down on her lap, listening attentively to some sound I could not hear. At her feet on the rug I would finish reading the paper and start to sketch out the battle plan for the lightning raid by the Underground on the key government points in Jerusalem. Even in my dreams I defeated enemies, and I carried on dreaming of wars for several years after that summer.

The FOD Organization that summer consisted of only three fighters: Ben Hur, the commander-in-chief and also head of the Special Branch for Internal Security and Interrogation. I was his second-in-command. Chita Reznik was a private and a leading contender for promotion when the organization expanded. Apart from being second-in-command, I was also regarded as the brains: it was I who founded the organization at the beginning of the summer holidays and gave it its name, FOD (short for 'Freedom Or Death'). It was my idea to collect nails, bend them, and scatter them on the approach road to the army camp so as to puncture the British tires. And I composed the slogans that Chita was ordered to paint in thick black letters on the walls of neighbouring houses: 'BRITS YOU'RE IN THE WRONG – GO BACK WHERE YOU BELONG!', 'WITH BLOOD FIRE AND SWEAT OUR FREEDOM WE'LL GET!' 'PERFIDIOUS ALBION, HANDS OFF ZION!' (I learnt the expression 'Perfidious Albion' from Father.) Our plan for the summer was to finish building our secret rocket. In a derelict hut on the edge of the wadi, behind Chita's backyard, we already had the electric motor from an old refrigerator, some parts from a motorbike, and several dozen yards of electric wire, fuses, a battery, bulbs, and six bottles of nail varnish, from which we planned to extract the acetone to make explosives. By the end of the summer the rocket would be finished and aimed precisely at the façade of Buckingham Palace where King George of England lived, and then we were going to send him a proud, firm letter: 'You have till the Day of Atonement to get out of our country, and if you don't, then our Day of Judgment will become your Day of Reckoning.'

What would the British have replied to this letter if we had only had another two or three weeks and managed to finish making our rocket? Perhaps they would have seen sense and cleared out, thus sparing themselves and us a good deal of blood and suffering. It's hard to know. But in the middle of the summer my secret relationship with Sergeant Dunlop was discovered. I had hoped it would last forever and never be found out. And because it was discovered the writing appeared on the wall and I received the order to appear that evening at the edge of the Tel Arza Woods, to face a court martial on a charge of treason.

The fact is I knew in advance that the trial would make no difference. No explanations or excuses would help me. As in all clandestine movements everywhere and at all times, anyone who is branded a traitor is a traitor and that's that. It's pointless to try to defend yourself.

5

BEN HUR WAS a foxlike boy; he was sharp and fair and skinny, with eyes that were almost khaki. I didn't like him. In fact, we weren't even friends. There was something else, something much closer than friendship. If Ben Hur had ordered me, say, to remove all the water in the Dead Sea to the Upper Galilee, bucket by bucket, I would have obeyed, so that when I had finished I might have a chance of hearing him say, out of the corner of his mouth, in that lazy drawl of his, the words 'You're OK, Proffy'. Ben Hur used words like someone throwing gravel at a streetlamp. He hardly parted his teeth when he spoke, as though he could not be bothered. Sometimes he pronounced the first *P* of Proffy with a kind of contemptuous little explosion: *P*roffy.

Ben Hur's sister, Yardena, played the clarinet. Once she cleaned up a cut on my knee and put a plaster on it, and I regretted not having a cut on my other knee, too. When I thanked her, she burst into tinkling laughter and turned to a non-existent audience: Look, a clam-boy. I didn't know what Yardena meant by calling me a clam-boy, but I already knew that one day I would know and that when I did it would turn out that I had always known. It's a complicated thing and I must try to find a simpler way to explain it. Maybe like this. I had a kind of shadow knowledge that sometimes comes long before knowledge itself. And it was precisely because of this shadow knowledge that I had a feeling that I was a low-down traitor that evening on the roof, when I accidentally saw her changing her clothes, and what I almost didn't see came back to me on many occasions: over and over again I almost didn't see it. I was so embarrassed that every time this happened I felt a shudder like you do when chalk scrapes on the blackboard, or like the sour taste of soap between your teeth, which is the taste a traitor has in his mouth at the moment of betrayal or soon afterwards. I wanted to write her a letter, to explain that I had had no intention whatsoever of spying on her, and to apologize. But how could I? Especially because from then on, every time I went back to my lookout on the roof, I was unable not to remember that the window was there, opposite, and that I mustn't look in that direction, even by accident, even against my will, even in passing, as I scanned the horizon from Mount Nebi Samwil towards Mount Scopus.

Ben Hur and I were joined by Chita Reznik, the boy with two fathers. (The first one was always away on trips and the other one would disappear from the house a few hours before the first got back. We all made fun of Chita, calling him Revolving Door and so on, and Chita used to join in the fun, laughing at his mother and his two fathers, playing the fool, giving a series of monkey imitations, making faces and uttering chimpanzee barks that somehow came out more like whimpers.) Chita Reznik was a slave-boy. He was always the one who ran to fetch balls that flew over the fence into the wadi. He always carried the piles of supplies when we set off for Tibet to hunt for the abominable snowman. He would fish matches, springs, shoelaces, a corkscrew, a penknife out of his pockets, anything you asked him for or that anyone needed. At the end of the great tank battles on the rug, Chita always stayed behind to pick up the dominoes and draughts counters and put them all away in their boxes.

We staged these tank battles nearly every morning, after my parents had left for work. We conducted extensive manoeuvres in readiness for the day when the British would leave and we would have to repel a co-ordinated attack by all the Arab armies. My father had a whole shelf of books on military history. With the help of these books and the big maps on the wall in the passage we re-enacted on the rug the toughest engagements at Dunkirk, Stalingrad, El-Alamein, Kursk and

J40729
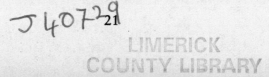
LIMERICK
COUNTY LIBRARY

21

the Ardennes, learning vital lessons for our own imminent war.

At eight o'clock in the morning, as soon as the door closed behind my mother and father, I would quickly tidy the kitchen, close the windows and shutters to keep the apartment cool and deter snoopers, and deploy the pieces on the rug in the opening positions of a crucial battle. I used buttons, matchsticks, dominoes, draughts counters and chessmen, pins with flags and coloured threads to mark borders and battle lines. I placed all the combat units of the various powers at their starting points. And I waited. Shortly before nine Ben Hur and Chita would knock at the door, first two quick, firm knocks and then, after a pause, a softer one. I identified them through the spyhole, and we exchanged passwords. Chita, outside, would ask 'Freedom?' and I, on the inside, would answer 'Or Death'.

Sometimes in the middle of a battle, Ben Hur would declare a break and then he would lead us in a raid on the icebox. I liked those mornings, especially those rare moments when Ben Hur uttered through pursed lips the words 'You're OK, Proffy'.

I did not know yet that these words are only worth anything when you say them to yourself. And in honesty.

By the time a quarter of the holiday had passed, we had made certain deductions about where Rommel and Zhukov, Montgomery and George Patton had gone wrong, and how we ourselves would avoid making the same mistakes when the moment came. We would take the big map of Palestine and its surroundings down off the wall, lay it on the rug, and practise driving the British out and repelling the combined Arab armies. Ben Hur was the commanding officer and I was the grey matter. Incidentally, even now as I write I have a wall in my home that is covered with maps. Sometimes I stand in front of them, put on my glasses (which are nothing like my father's round ones), and follow the course of the war in Bosnia or Azerbaijan as described in the news on the wireless or in the papers. There is always a war going on somewhere in the world. Sometimes I suspect, from looking at the map, that one of the sides has made a mistake, has failed to notice an opportunity to pull off a surprise outflanking movement.

By the middle of the summer I was preparing plans for a Hebrew Armada, with destroyers, submarines, frigates and aircraft carriers. I was planning to investigate the possibility of a co-ordinated lightning strike on the British naval bases all round the shores of the Mediterranean, in Port Said, Famagusta, Malta, Mersa Matruh, Gibraltar. Only not here, in Haifa, because they would obviously be expecting something here. Were there any other British bases in the Mediterranean basin? I was planning to put this question to Sergeant Dunlop at our next meeting in the Orient Palace Café. I could ask him with apparently innocent curiosity the sort of question you might expect to hear from a child who was interested in geography. But on second thoughts I dropped the idea, for fear that simply putting the question might arouse suspicion, and thus jeopardize the element of surprise that was vital to the success of our plan.

Better to ask Father.

But in fact there was no need to ask anyone. I could check it for myself. I could correlate information freely available in the encyclopedia with other information freely available on the maps in the atlas. The correlation of freely available sources can sometimes yield valuable secret information. (I still believe this. Sometimes I put an ostensibly innocent question to somebody, such as, What is your favourite view? And later on in the conversation, after half an hour or so I casually ask what he or she wanted to be when they grew up. I compare the two answers in my mind, and I know.)

The Hebrew Armada never put to sea, and now it never would. Instead, I was to face a court martial on a charge of low-down treason and passing secrets to the enemy.

I thought to myself: You could even call Robin Hood a traitor. However, only a petty person would concern himself with that aspect of Robin Hood. Even though it did exist. It's a fact.

But what is treachery really?

I sat on my father's chair. I switched on the desk lamp. I took an oblong card from the pile. I wrote on it something like this: 'Check whether there is any connection between the word *boged*, "traitor", and the word *beged*, "clothing". Cf. "a wolf in sheep's clothing".' A traitor covers things up, just as clothes do. And clothes get torn just when you least expect it. Also, if you put warm clothes on, there's a heat wave, and if you dress for the hot weather suddenly it's freezing cold. (Though in point of fact the treachery here is due to the weather, not to the clothes.) In Bible class with Mr Zerubbabel Gihon we studied a verse from Job: 'My brethren have dealt treacherously as a river.' Not the peaceful rivers of the Ukraine that Mother talks about so wistfully, but the rivers here in the Land of Israel: treacherous rivers. In the heat of summer, when you are thirsty, they give you burning gravel instead of water, whereas in winter, when you are walking along the river bed, they suddenly flood. The Prophet Jeremiah laments: 'For the house of Israel and the house of Judah have dealt very treacherously against me, said the Lord.' And Jeremiah, too, was called a traitor: they tried him and found him guilty and threw him in a pit.

Whereas the expression 'low-down', I noted on another card, means vile or base. Low can mean low-spirited, gloomy or depressed. It is related to lowly, meaning pitiful or humble. Or mean. So is low the opposite of proud or arrogant? Ben Hur Tykocinski is arrogant, but he is also mean. (And how about me: I didn't have the courage to write to Yardena and apologize for peeping at her.) I must ask Sergeant Dunlop how you say 'low-down traitor' in English and whether English also has a connection between treachery and clothing and between baseness and humility.

Will I ever see him again?

Asking myself this question made me miss him. Naturally I never forgot for a moment that he belonged to the opposite side, to the enemy. But he was not a private enemy, although he was private. He was mine.

I can't put it off any longer. I must talk now about Sergeant Dunlop and about our relationship. Even though it's hard for me to do so.

6

WE USED TO meet secretly three or four times a week in the back room of the Orient Palace Café. Despite its name, this was actually a run-down tin shack covered with a dense jungle of passionflower, in a little alley to the west of the army camp. In the front room there was a billiard table covered in green baize, which was always surrounded by a perspiring group of English soldiers and policemen and a few Jerusalem youths with smart shirts and ties, Jews, Arabs, Greeks, Armenians, with gold rings and greased-down hair, as well as two or three girls wafting on clouds of perfume. I never lingered in this front room: I reminded myself that I was here on a mission. I never peeped in the direction of the barmaid. Everybody who spoke to her tried to make her laugh, and nearly everybody succeeded. She had a habit of leaning forward as if she was bowing whenever she pushed a glass of frothy beer to the front of the bar, and as she did so a deep cavern opened up in the top of her dress, and some people might have found it hard not to look but I never so much as glanced at her.

I would hurriedly cross this front room, which was full of laughter and smoke and go on into the inner room, which was quieter and had only four or five tables, covered with oilcloth printed with flowers and Greek ruins. Young men sometimes sat here playing backgammon, sometimes a couple or two sat close together, but unlike the outer room, people here spoke in whispers. Sergeant Dunlop and I used to sit for an hour or an hour and a half at the table in the corner, with several books open in front of us: a Hebrew Bible, a pocket dictionary, a first English reader. Now that more than forty-five years have gone by, and Britain is no longer an enemy, and the Hebrew State exists, now that Ben Hur Tykocinski is called Mr Benny Takin and owns a chain of hotels, and Chita Reznik earns his living repairing solar water heaters, and I still chase words and put them in their proper places, I may as well write this: I betrayed no secrets to Stephen Dunlop. Not a single one, not even a little one. I didn't even tell him my name. Right to the end. All I did was to read the Bible with him in Hebrew and teach him some modern words that are not in the Bible, and in exchange he helped me to learn the rudiments of English. He was a perplexed and, by his own account, lonely man. He was a large, broad man, pink-faced, spongelike, a bit of a gossip, and he blushed a lot. His legs below his shorts seemed pudgy and hairless, with little wrinkles like those you see on the limbs of a baby who has not yet learned to walk.

Sergeant Dunlop had brought with him from Canterbury, his home town, a kind of Hebrew that he had learned from his uncle the vicar. (His brother, Jeremy Dunlop, was also in the church: he was a missionary in Malaya.) His Hebrew was soft, like cartilage, as though it had no bones. He had no friends, he claimed. ('Neither have I enemies or foes', he added without my asking.) He was serving in the British Police in Jerusalem as an accountant and pay clerk. Occasionally, when there was an emergency, he would be sent to guard a government office for half a night or to check identity cards at a roadblock. I recorded all these details in my memory the moment they came out of his mouth. In the evening, when I was at home, I wrote it all down in a notebook to swell the information stored at the FOD Organization headquarters. Sergeant Dunlop was fond of retailing little items of gossip about his friends and superiors: which one was a miser, a dandy, a sycophant, who had recently changed his aftershave, which high-ranking CID officer had to use a special anti-dandruff shampoo. All these details made him giggle, which embarrassed him, but he still found it hard to stop. Major Bentley had bought a silver bracelet for Colonel Parker's secretary. Lady Nolan had a new cook. Mrs Sherwood left the room in disgust every time Captain Bolder came in.

I tut-tutted politely and imprinted it all in my memory. And my heart slunk barefoot, on tiptoe, a beggar among dukes and earls, with eyes gaping in amazement, through high-ceilinged, mahogany-panelled rooms lit by chandeliers, watching Captain Bolder entering proudly and the beautiful Mrs Sherwood immediately turning on her heel and flouncing out.

Apart from the language of the Prophets, Sergeant Dunlop also knew Latin and some Greek, and in his spare time he was teaching himself literary Arabic ('that the three sons of Noah – Shem Ham and Japheth – may dwell together in my heart, as it was before the division of tongues'). He pronounced the name Ham like the English word ham, instead of with the Hebrew guttural *h* sound, and noticing me stifling my amusement, he said, 'I speak as I may speak.' I could not stop myself confiding in him that my father also knew Latin and Greek, and other languages besides. Then I felt sorry and ashamed of myself, because we must under no circumstances communicate even innocent information like that to them: it is impossible to know what use they might make of it. After all, the British, too, can collate one freely available fact with another and come up with a secret that they can exploit to our disadvantage.

Now I must explain how Sergeant Dunlop and I became acquainted. We met as enemies. Pursuer and pursued. Policeman and Underground fighter.

7

LATE ONE AFTERNOON at the beginning of the summer holidays I set out on my own to investigate possible hiding places in the caves behind Sanhedriya. In one of the caves my search revealed a small chamber almost entirely blocked up with a heap of stones and dust. A superficial exploration brought to light four cartridge cases from rifle bullets, and I made up my mind that it was my duty to carry on searching. When it grew dark and a coldness like the touch of a corpse wafted towards me out of the depth of the cave, I came out. Night had fallen. The curfew had emptied the streets. My heart thumped panic-stricken in my chest as though it were trying to punch out a little space behind itself that it could hide in.

I decided to creep home through the backyards. Since early spring, the FOD had devised a network of crossings from one yard to the next. Following a directive I had received from Ben Hur and transmitted, after working on it and improving it, as an order to Chita Reznik, Chita had laid out pathways of planks, stones, crates, and ropes, linking up strategic points. So we could get over fences and walls and sally forth or retreat through the maze of backyards and gardens.

Suddenly a single shot rang out not far away. A real shot: sharp, savage, and terrifying.

My shirt stuck to my skin with fear. The blood throbbed in my temples and my neck like a tom-tom. Panting and terrified I started running monkey-like, bent double, over fences and through bushes, grazing my knees, hitting my shoulder against a stone wall, catching the turnup of my shorts on a wire fence but not stopping to loosen it: like a lizard shedding its tail I dragged myself free, leaving a tatter of cloth and a shred of torn skin in the fence's grip.

I had just emerged from the back steps of the post office, whose dark windows were protected by grilles, and was on the point of slipping diagonally across Zephaniah Street, when a dazzling beam of light suddenly hit me in the eyes and in the same instant something cold and soft and moist, like the touch of a frog, made contact with my back and groped its way up my spine and into my hair. I froze, like a hare in the split second before the predator's claws strike. The hand that was clutching my hair was not strong, but big and soft, like a jellyfish. So was the voice behind the blinding light: not the usual British bark but a single porridge-like syllable: 'Halt!' Then at once, in classroom Hebrew but with a rounded English accent: 'Whither dost thou hasten?'

It was a clumsy, rather feeble British policeman. A metal badge bearing his identification number shone on each shoulder. His cap was askew. We were both panting hoarsely. Our faces were dripping sweat. He was wearing khaki shorts that reached down to his knees and khaki socks that reached up to his knees. Between the two his knees gleamed faintly in the dark; they looked plump and soft.

'Please, sir,' I said in the language of the enemy. 'Please, kindly sir, let me go home.'

He answered, again in Hebrew. Not in our kind of Hebrew, though. He said:

'Let not the lad go astray in the darkness.'

Then he said he would take me to my front door, and that I must show him the way.

I should not really have done it, because our policy was to disobey all their orders and so to impede the motion of their repressive machinery. But what alternative did I have? His hand was on my shoulder. Up to that evening, I had never laid hands on an Englishman and no Englishman had laid hands on me. I had often read in the papers about the hand of the British. For instance: 'Hands off our survivors.' Or: 'May the arrogant hand raised against the last of our hope be lopped off!' Or: 'Cursed be the hand that shakes hands with our oppressors.'

And here was the hand of the enemy on my shoulder, and it was like cotton-wool. I felt ashamed, as though I was being touched by a girl. (At that time, I held to the view that when a girl touches a boy it humiliates the boy. A boy touching a girl, on the other hand, was an act of heroism that could only happen in a dream, or in the movies. And if it did happen in a dream it was best not to remember.) I wanted to tell the British policeman to take his hand off the scruff of my neck, but I didn't know how to. And I wasn't entirely sure I wanted to, because the street was empty and sinister, and the buildings were dark and shuttered like sunken wrecks. The dark air seemed thick and menacing. The plump English policeman was lighting the way with his torch, and I had a feeling that the beam of light on the pavement ahead of us offered some protection against the evil that lurked in the empty city. He said:

'Lo, I am Mr Stephen Dunlop. I am an Englishman, who would give all the substance of his house for the language of the Prophets and whose heart is in thrall to the Chosen People.'

'Tank you, kindly sir,' I said, as we had been taught at school, and I felt ashamed of myself. I was glad that nobody would ever find out. I was also ashamed of myself because I had forgotten that you were supposed to pronounce the first consonant of 'thank you' with your tongue between your teeth, to make that special British sound that was halfway between *t* and *s*. To my shame, I had said 'tank' instead of 'thank'.

'My home is in the city of Canterbury, my heart is in the city of Jerusalem and speedily shall my days in Jerusalem be ended and I shall arise and return to my land just as I came hither.'

Against the urgings of my conscience, against my principles, against my better judgment, I was suddenly quite taken by him. (Is such a British policeman, who sides with us even though it is against the orders of his king, to be considered a traitor?) In the three poems I had written about the heroes of the time of King David and shown to Yardena alone, I too had chosen to use exalted language. Actually he was very lucky,

30

that sergeant, that it was me he caught that night in the street and not Ben Hur or Chita: they would have made fun of his highfalutin Hebrew. Nevertheless, a sober voice inside me whispered: Better watch out for them. Don't be too gullible. As we learned from Mr Zerubbabel Gihon: 'They are haughty and they speak hard things, for there are seven abominations in their heart', 'full of guile and deceit' (and what is 'guile' actually?), 'their hands are full of blood'. And, of course, there was Father's invariable expression, the one from the slogans he composed in English for the Underground: Perfidious Albion.

I am ashamed to write this, but I shall write it none the less: I could easily have run away. I could have slipped out of his grasp and vanished into a yard. The policeman was clumsy, inattentive, he reminded me rather of my teacher Mr Gihon: perplexed but well-meaning. Even the slight slope of Zephaniah Street had him panting and wheezing. (Later on I found out that he suffered from asthma.) Not only could I have escaped; but if I had really been a panther in the basement, it would have been simple to snatch his pistol, which instead of hanging in its rightful place, on his hip, had slipped round his belt to his bottom, where it swayed and slapped the Sergeant lightly with every step he took, like a door that is not properly closed. It was my clear duty to grab the gun and make a dash for it. Or to snatch it, point it at him, straight between his eyes (I think he was also shortsighted), and shout in English 'Hands up!', or, better still, 'Don't move!' (Gary Cooper, Clark Gable, Humphrey Bogart, any of them would have easily got the better, single-handed, of fifty such cotton-wool enemies.) But instead of overpowering him and gaining a precious gun for our nation, I confess that I suddenly felt rather sorry that the way home was not a little longer. And at the same time I felt that it was a disgrace to feel like that and that I ought to feel ashamed. And I really did feel ashamed.

The sergeant said in his spongey accent:

'In the book of the Prophet Samuel it is written "And the lad was only a lad". Pray fear no evil. I am a stranger that loveth Israel.'

I weighed his words. I decided that it was my duty to tell

him the simple, honest truth, in my name and in the name of the nation. This is what I said (in English):

'Don't angry on me please sir. We are enimies until you give back our land.'

What if he arrested me for speaking these bold words? Never mind, I thought. They won't scare me with their prisons and their scaffolds and their gallows. I ran over in my mind the rules we had learned from Ben Hur Tykocinski in the general HQ meeting: four ways of withstanding interrogation under torture.

In the dark I could feel Sergeant Dunlop's smile on my face, like the slobbering tongue of a clumsy, good-natured dog:

'Soon may all the dwellers in Jerusalem have tranquillity. Peace be within her walls, and prosperity within her palaces. In English speech, young man, we say enemies, not enimies. Is it thy desire that we should continue to see each other's face and learn together each one the other's tongue? And what is thy name, young man?'

In a flash, coolly and clearheadedly, I took stock of the situation from every angle. I had learned from Father that in a time of testing an intelligent man should locate all the data at his disposal within an overall picture, distinguish rationally between what is possible and what is necessary, and always weigh up coolly the various options open to him; only then should he choose the lesser evil. (Father often used not only the expressions 'definitely', 'indubitably', but also 'rationally' and 'genuinely'.) In that instant I remembered the night when the clandestine immigrants were being landed. How the heroes of the Underground carried the survivors on their backs from the beached ship. How a whole British brigade surrounded them on the beach. How the heroes of the Underground destroyed their identity papers and mingled with the immigrants so that the British would not be able to tell who was a resident and who should be expelled as an illegal immigrant. How the British cooped them all up with coils of barbed wire and interrogated them one by one, name, address, occupation, and to all the interrogators' questions they all, immigrants and resistance fighters alike, gave the same proud reply: I am a Jew from the Land of Israel.

At that moment I too made up my mind not to tell them my name. Even if they tortured me. Nevertheless, out of tactical considerations, I chose at that juncture to pretend I had not understood the question. The sergeant repeated gently:

'If it is thy wish, let us see each other from time to time at the Orient Palace Café. That is where I spend my spare time: I shall learn Hebrew from thy mouth and recompense thee with lessons in English. The name is Mr Stephen Dunlop. And thou, my young man?'

'I'm Proffy.' And I added boldly: 'A Jew from the Land of Israel.'

What did I care? Proffy was only a nickname. In a film I remembered – I think it was *Lightning Bolt* with Olivia de Havilland and Humphrey Bogart – Humphrey Bogart was captured by the enemy. Wounded, unshaven, with his clothes torn, and a thin trickle of blood trailing from the corner of his mouth, he confronted his interrogators with a faint smile that was polite yet mocking. His cool manner expressed a subtle contempt that his captors did not and could not grasp.

Sergeant Dunlop may not have understood why I said 'a Jew from the Land of Israel' instead of giving him my name. But he did not protest. His soft hand moved for a moment from my back to the scruff of my neck, gave me a couple of light pats, and settled again on my shoulder. My father rarely put his hand on my shoulder. His purpose in doing so was to say: Think again, weigh it up rationally, yes indeed, and kindly change your mind. Whereas Sergeant Dunlop's hand was saying to me, more or less, that on a dark night like this it was better for two people to be together, even if they were enemies.

Father used to say about the British: 'Those arrogant swashbucklers who behave as if they own the world.' My mother once said: 'They're nothing but young men who are full of beer and homesickness. Hungry for a woman and a holiday.' (I knew and I didn't know what 'hungry for a woman' meant. I didn't see that it was any reason to forgive them. And definitely not a reason to forgive women. On the contrary.)

Under the streetlamp on the corner of Zephaniah Street and

Amos Street we stopped to let the policeman draw breath. He stood fanning his sweaty face with his cap. All of a sudden he put the cap on my head, chuckled, and put it back on his own head. For a moment he looked like a rubber doll that had been inflated. He looked nothing like a swashbuckler. And yet I did not forget that I mustn't not think of him as a swashbuckler.

He said:

'I was somewhat short of breath.'

I seized the opportunity at once to repay him for correcting my English earlier. I said:

'In Hebrew we don't say I was short of breath sir. We say my breath was short.'

Removing his hand from my shoulder he pulled out a chequered handkerchief and wiped the sweat off his forehead. It was the perfect moment for me to run away. Or to snatch the gun. Why did I stand there like a dummy, in the empty night, on the corner of Zephaniah and Amos Streets, waiting for him, as though he were an absentminded uncle that I'd been told to accompany in case he forgot where he was going? Why did I have an urge at that moment, when the sergeant was 'somewhat short of breath', to run and fetch him a glass of water? If the sign of treachery is a sour taste or a sensation of having your teeth set on edge, like when you chew lemon peel or soap, or when chalk squeaks on the blackboard, then at that moment I may already have been a bit of a traitor. Although I can't deny that there was also a kind of secret enjoyment. Now that I am writing this story, more than forty-five years later, and the Hebrew State exists and has conquered its enemies over and over again, I still have an urge to skip over that moment.

On the other hand, I look back on it fondly.

I have already written both here and in other places that everything has at least two sides (except a shadow). I remember with amazement that in that strange moment there was deep darkness all around us and a little island of faint light trembling beneath the policeman's torch, and there was a frightening emptiness, and a lot of restless shadows. But Sergeant Dunlop and I were not a shadow. And my not running away was not a shadow but a not-running-away. And a not-snatching-the-gun. At that instant a decision formed itself, as though a bell had rung inside me:

Yes indeed.

Definitely.

And decidedly.

I would take up his suggestion.

I would meet him at the Orient Palace, and then, under the guise of swapping English and Hebrew lessons, I would cunningly extract from him vital classified information about the deployment of the enemy troops and the schemes of the repressive regime. By doing this I would be a thousand times more useful to the Underground than by running away or even by snatching a single pistol. Henceforth I was a spy. A mole. A secret agent disguised as a child interested in the English language. From this moment on I would act as in a game of chess.

8

FATHER STOOD IN the doorway and said in his slow English, with his Russian *r*s that sounded like roller skates scraping over a rough pavement:

'Thank you, officer, for bringing us back our stray lamb. We were beginning to be worried. Particularly my wife. We are most grateful.'

'Dad,' I whispered, 'he's all right. He likes Jews. Give him a glass of water and watch out, he understands Hebrew.'

My father didn't hear. Or else he decided to take no notice. He said:

'And as for the little scamp, don't worry, sir, we will deal with him. Thank you once again. And goodbye, or *shalom*, peace, as we Jews have been accustomed to say for thousands of years, and we still mean it, despite all we have undergone.'

Sergeant Dunlop replied in English, but changed to Hebrew halfway through:

'The lad and I were talking on the way. He's a dear, bright lad. Don't be too hard on him. With your permission I, too, will use the Hebrew word *shalom*. Peace. "Peace, peace to him that is near, and to him that is far off."' And all of a sudden he offered me his plump hand that my shoulder had grown accustomed to and still wanted. And, winking, he added in a whisper:

'Orient Palace. Six o'clock tomorrow.'

I said goodbye. Thank you. My heart rebuked me: Shame on you, hellenizer, lackey, coward, bootlicker, why in heaven's name are you saying thank you to him? Suddenly a wave of self-respect swept through me like the brandy that my father once let me sip to cure me of ever wanting it again. Everything I had ever been taught about generations of down-trodden Jews, and Humphrey Bogart the proud captive, all stuck in my throat, and I thrust my clenched hand deep into my pocket. I left the enemy's hand hanging surprised in mid-air, until he had to give in and convert the handshake into a kind of feeble wave. He tipped his head and left. My dignity was intact. So why did I feel once again that taste of treachery in my mouth, as though I had been chewing soap?

9

FATHER CLOSED THE door. Still standing in the hallway, he said to my mother:

'Please keep out of this.'

And quietly he asked me:

'What do you have to say for yourself?'

'I was late. I'm sorry. The curfew started. I was already on my way home when that policeman caught me.'

'You were late. Why were you late?'

'I was late. I'm sorry.'

'So am I,' said Father sadly, adding: 'Yes indeed. I am sorry too.'

Mother said:

'There was an incident in Haifa. A boy of your age was out in the curfew. The English caught him, accused him of sticking up bills, sentenced him to fifteen strokes. Of the lash. Two days later his parents found him in some Arab hospital, and his back I don't want to describe what state –'

Father said to her:

'Would you please let me finish.'

And to me he said:

'Yes indeed. Kindly take note: you are not to leave your room till the end of this week except to go to the bathroom. So you will have supper on your own. That way you will have plenty of free time to reflect honestly on what happened and also on what might have happened. Added to which Your Lordship will have to contend with an economic crisis, because your pocket money is frozen until the first of

September. Besides which, the aquarium and the trip to Talpiot are definitely out of the question. Wait. We haven't finished yet. Lights-out this week is put forward from a quarter past ten to nine o'clock. Your Excellency undoubtedly understands the connection: it is so that you can ponder on your behaviour in the dark. It has been definitely established that, in the dark, a rational man reasons with himself far more thoroughly than with the light on. That is all. Your Lordship will kindly take to your room this instant. Yes indeed. Without any supper. No, I must ask you once again not to interfere: this is between me and him.'

AFTER I WAS released from house arrest, I suggested to Ben Hur that he call a staff meeting at the FOD HQ in our hide-out in the Tel Arza Woods. Without going into details I reported on my discovery of a vital source of intelligence and requested authorization to proceed with an espionage assignment. Chita Reznik said:

'Oho!'

Ben Hur shot Chita a foxy khaki look and said neither yes nor no, and did not look at me. Finally he addressed his fingernails:

'The High Command must be kept in the picture at all times.'

I interpreted these words as a specific authorization to undertake the mission. I said:

'Definitely. Once there is a picture, that is.' And I pointed out that even in *Panther in the Basement* Tyrone Power was given a free hand, wasn't he, to disappear in the fog and assume and discard identities at his sole discretion. Chita said:

'That's right. And he turned into a diamond smuggler and then into a circus owner.'

'A circus,' Ben Hur said. 'That's just right for Proffy. I'm not so sure about the panther in the basement, though.'

I never imagined that I would be put under surveillance. That the internal security squad would swing into action that very day: Ben Hur hated not knowing. He had an unquench-able thirst. There was a hint of thirst in his face, his move-ments, his voice. For example, when we played football (he was the right half, I was the commentator), we were amazed during halftime to see how Ben Hur could down six or seven glasses of fizzy lemonade one after the other, then drink water from the tap and at the end still look thirsty. Always. I can't explain it. Not long ago I bumped into him as we were waiting for an El-Al flight; he was wearing a business suit and crocodile-skin shoes, with an expensive raincoat folded over his arm, and a travelling bag festooned with buckles, displaying a patent name in silver letters. He's not called Ben Hur Tykocinski any more; his name is Mr Benny Takin, and he owns a chain of hotels, but he still looks thirsty.

Thirsty for what? I wish I knew.

It may be that such people are condemned to wander forever in an inner desert, with arid yellow dunes, shifting sands, a wilderness. Many waters cannot quench it, neither can the floods drown it. To this day I am fascinated by people like that, just as I was when I was a child. But with the passage of the years I have learned to beware of them. Or, rather, not so much to beware of them as to beware of being fascinated by them.

11

THAT FRIDAY AFTERNOON I slipped away to the Orient Palace Café. As I have already said, despite its name this was actually a dilapidated shack half-buried in a tangle of passionflower. It wasn't even in the east: it was in the west of Jerusalem, in one of those little lanes of slouchy old German villas behind the army camp, on the way to Romema. These secretive, thick-walled houses had arched windows, tiled roofs, cellars and attics, water cisterns, and walled gardens whose leafy trees cast a gentle, foreign shade in the courtyards, as though you had reached the frontiers of a promised land whose inhabitants led quiet, peaceable lives, a promised land you could only see from a distance but never enter.

On my way to the Orient Palace I made various detours through backyards, across empty lots, and, to be on the safe side, I made a further loop to the south round the Takhkemoni School. Every now and again I took a quick look over my shoulder to make sure that I had managed to shake off anyone who might be shadowing me. I also wanted to make the journey longer because I had never accepted that a straight line is the shortest distance between two points. I said to myself:

Straight line: so what?

During the time I was in detention in my room, in the dark, I had used my mind just as my father had asked me: I had reassessed every step, false or not, that I had taken the night I was caught by the English policeman. And I had come to certain conclusions. First, there was no doubt that my parents were right about my being late. It was a pointless risk. No clever resistance fighter gets into a confrontation with the enemy unless it is on his own initiative and with the objective of securing an advantage. Any contact between the enemy and the resistance that is not initiated by the latter only benefits the enemy. I had taken an unnecessary risk by staying in the Sanhedriya caves until after the curfew had begun, because I was dreaming dreams. A true resistance fighter must subjugate even his dreams to the pursuit of victory. At a time when the fate of the nation hung in the balance, dreaming for its own sake was a luxury that only girls might perhaps indulge in. A fighter must be on his guard, especially against dreaming about Yardena, who, although she was almost twenty, still had a girlish habit of arranging the hem of her skirt after she sat down, as if her knees were a baby that needed to be covered up properly, not too little so as to catch cold and not too much so that it will not be able to breathe. And when she played the clarinet it was as though the music came not from the instrument but straight out of her body, only passing through the clarinet to pick up some sweetness and sadness, and taking you to a real, silent place where there is no enemy, no struggle, and where everything is free from shame and treachery and clear of thoughts of betrayal.

That's enough, idiot.

With such thoughts I reached the Orient Palace, with one voice pleading with me to turn round and go home before I got into deep trouble, and another making fun of me for being a scaredy-cat, and a third, which was less a voice than a steel vice, pulling me inside. So I slipped into the bar, avoiding the billiard players in the front room and hoping they did not notice me, suppressing the urge to touch the green baize with my fingertips. (To this day I find it hard when I see baize to resist feeling its softness.) A couple of British soldiers with red berets, the sort we called 'poppies', their tommy guns hanging from their shoulders, were chatting softly with the barmaid, who laughed as she leaned forward to give them the tankards of frothy beer and a good look at her cleavage, but I didn't spare her a glance. I crossed the smoke and the smell of beer and intrigues and made it safely to the back room. At the far end of this room, behind a table covered with flowery oilcloth, I spotted my man. He was not quite as I remembered him. He was stranger, more serious, more British. He was sitting bent over a book; his thick thighs were crossed, and his uniform was crumpled and untidy. He wore wide khaki shorts down to his knees, and a wide wrinkled shirt of greenish khaki (as opposed to the yellowish khaki of local manufacture that my father wore). On his shoulders I could see the silvery glint of his policeman's number, which I had memorized on the first night: 4479. An easy, pleasant number. His pistol had slipped round to his backside again, squashed between that and the back of the chair. In front of him on the table I could see an open Bible, a dictionary, a glass of yellowish lemonade that had lost its fizz, two more books, an exercise book, a scrumpled handkerchief, and an open packet of sweets. As he looked up and beamed at me his face looked pink and slack, as though he had too much skin, which had a slightly unhealthy hue, like melted vanilla ice-cream. His cap, the one he had placed briefly on my head that night, was lying at the edge of the table, looking more authoritative and official than Sergeant Dunlop himself. His hair was brown and thinning, and he had a ruler-sharp parting right in the middle of his head, like the watershed we had been learning about in geography.

From his vague smile I realized that he had forgotten me.

'Hello, Sergeant Dunlop,' I said in Hebrew.

He went on smiling, but started to blink a little.

'It's me. From the curfew. You arrested me in the street and took me home and released me. You suggested we should teach each other Hebrew and English, sir. So here I am.'

Sergeant Dunlop reddened and said:

'Oh. Ah.'

He still didn't remember a thing. So I reminded him:

'"Let not the lad go astray in the darkness." Don't you remember, sir? About a week ago. You say enemies not enimies?'

'Oh. Ah. So it is thou. Sit down. And what is thy wish this time?'

'You suggested we should study together. Hebrew and English. I'm ready.'

'Oh. So. Thou camest according to thy promise. Blessed is he that waiteth and cometh.'

And that is how our lessons began. By the second meeting I had agreed that he should order me a lemonade, even though in principle we shouldn't accept anything from them, not a thread or a shoelace. But I weighed it up and decided that it was my duty to gain his confidence and dispel any hint of suspicion from his mind, so that I could get him to utter the information we needed. And that is the only reason I forced myself to take a few sips of the lemonade he bought me, and also accepted a couple of wafer biscuits.

We read a few chapters together from Samuel and Kings. We discussed them in modern Hebrew, which Sergeant Dunlop hardly recognized. The words for crane, pencil, shirt filled him with wonder because they have grown out of ancient words. Meanwhile I learned from him that English has a tense that has no equivalent in Hebrew, the present continuous, in which every verb ends with a sound like the touch of glass on glass: ing. In fact the ring of glass on glass helped me to understand this English tense: I imagined a light clink of glasses and with it a faint chime of this continuous present, moving further and further away, weakening, growing fainter and fainter, fading in the distance with a delightful continuousness that was pleasant to listen to, right to the end, without turning to any other activity while the sound was dimming, disappearing, dissipating and fading. Such listening could fittingly be called a continuous present.

When I told Sergeant Dunlop about the sound of glass that helped me to grasp the continuous present, he tried to praise me but he got in a muddle and uttered some English words that I did not fully understand. What I did understand was that, like everyone on our side, he found it easier to express ideas than feelings. I, too, had a feeling at that moment (a mixture of affection and shyness), but I stifled it because an enemy is an enemy and because I was not a girl. (So? What about girls? What have they got that draws us so? Not like glass on glass, more like a line of light on glass? And until when is it forbidden? Until we are grown up? Until there are no enemies left?) After the third or fourth meeting we shook

45

hands, because spies are allowed to and because I had managed to teach Sergeant Dunlop the difference between the silent and the mobile *shva* in Hebrew. I had never been a teacher, yet here was the Sergeant calling me a brilliant teacher, and I was pleased, but nevertheless I said, 'You're exaggerating, sir.' (I had to explain the Hebrew word for 'exaggerate', because it's not in the Bible. Though there is a kind of locust or grasshopper that has a similar name. I must check whether there's any connection.)

Sergeant Dunlop was a patient, slightly absentminded teacher, but when we swapped roles he became a quiet, attentive pupil. When he was writing Hebrew he concentrated so hard that his tongue stuck out of the corner of his mouth, like a baby's. Once he muttered 'Christ', but immediately corrected himself in embarrassment and said in Hebrew, 'God Almighty'. I had a special reason to shake his hand warmly at the end of the fourth lesson, because I had managed to extract a precious piece of information from him.

'Ere the summer shall cease,' he said, 'I shall arise and return to the land of my birth, for the days of our unit in Jerusalem shall speedily come to an end.'

I tried to conceal my excitement under a mask of politeness as I inquired:

'What is your unit?'

'Jerusalem Police. Northern Division. Section Nine. Speedily shall the British depart from the land. We are wearied. Our day is reaching its evening.'

'But when?'

'According to the time of life, perhaps.'

What a stroke of blessed luck, I thought, that it's me here and not Chita or Ben Hur, because they would never have known that 'according to the time of life' means exactly one more year. And so they would have failed to discover a vital military secret. It was my duty to communicate it with lightning speed to the FOD and even to the real Underground. (But how? Via my father? Or Yardena?) My heart sang in my chest like a panther in a basement. Never before had I done such a wonderfully helpful thing and perhaps I never would again. And yet almost at the same instant I tasted in my mouth the

46

sour, nauseous taste of low-down treachery: a shudder as from the sound of scraping chalk.

'And what will happen after the British evacuation, Sergeant Dunlop?'

'It's all written in the Good Book. "For I will defend this city, to save it." "The adversary and the enemy shall not enter into the gates of this city." "There shall yet old men and old women dwell in the streets of Jerusalem, and the streets of the city shall be full of boys and girls playing."'

How could I imagine that these meetings had already brought me under suspicion? That the Internal Security squad of the FOD High Command was watching my every move? I felt not a shadow of anxiety. I was convinced that Ben Hur and Chita were happy with my angling. Until one morning Chita, on Ben Hur's orders, painted on the wall of our house the words I mentioned at the beginning of my story, which I find it hard to repeat. And at lunchtime I found a note under the door: I was to appear in the Tel Arza Woods, to be interrogated, to stand trial for treachery. Instead of a panther in the basement, they saw me as a snake in the grass.

12

AT NIGHT, AFTER lights-out, I used to lie in the dark listening. Outside, on the other side of the wall, an empty, sinister world began. Even our familiar garden, with the pomegranate tree and the village I had built out of matchboxes underneath it, was not ours at night: it belonged to the curfew and to evil. From garden to garden groups of fighters advanced in the darkness on desperate missions. British patrols armed with searchlights and tracker dogs roamed the empty streets. Spies, detectives and traitors were pitted in a war of brains. Casting their nets. Planning cunning ambushes. The empty pavements were lit by a ghostly light from streetlamps wreathed in summer mist. Beyond our street, beyond the confines of our neighbourhood, lay more and more deserted streets, lanes, alleys, steps, archways, all pervaded by the darkness that was full of eyes, and pierced by the barking of dogs. Even the row of buildings on the other side of the road seemed on those nights of curfew to be cut off from us by a river of deep darkness. As though the Dorzions, Mrs Ostrowska, Dr Gryphius, Ben Hur and his sister Yardena were all on the other side of mountains of darkness. Beyond the same dark mountain were the Shibboleth newsstand and the Sinopsky Brothers grocery, protected by iron shutters and two padlocks. I felt that the phrase 'beyond the same dark mountain' could be felt with your fingertips like thick black baize. Above our heads Mr Lazarus's roof was swathed in darkness and the hens were pressed close together. On those nights all the hills that surrounded Jerusalem were mountains of darkness. And what was there beyond the hills? Stone-built villages, clustering around minarets. Empty valleys where foxes and jackals roamed and even the occasional hyena. Bloodthirsty gangs. And angry ghosts from bygone days.

I lay huddled, wide awake, until the silence became more heavily charged than it could bear, and then it began to be pierced by shots. Sometimes it was a distant stray burst of fire from the direction of Wadi Joz or Isawiya. At others a sharp, knife-like salvo maybe from Sheikh Jarrah or staccato machine-gun fire from Sanhedriya. Was it us? The real Underground? Brave lads flashing signals to each other from rooftop to rooftop with faint pocket torches? Sometimes, after midnight, a succession of heavy explosions came from the south of the city, from the direction of the German Colony or further still from the Valley of Hinnom or Abu Tor or the Allenby Camp or the hills of Mar Ilias on the way to Bethlehem. A dim rumble rolled through the thickness of the ground under the asphalt of the roads and the foundations of the buildings making the windowpanes chatter, and rising up from the floor into my bed producing a cold shudder.

The only telephone in the vicinity was at the pharmacy. Sometimes late at night I seemed to hear repeated ringing from three streets away, a pleading sound out there where there was not a living soul. And the closest wireless was in Dr Buster's apartment, six buildings eastwards. We would know nothing until dawn broke. Not even if the British tiptoed out of Jerusalem and left us on our own surrounded by masses of Arabs. Not even if hordes of armed marauders forced their way into the city. Not even if the Underground stormed Government House.

Through the other wall, from my parents' bedroom, I could hear only silence. My mother might have been reading, in her dressing gown, or writing out a shopping list for the institute where she worked. My father would sit up till one, sometimes two o'clock, his back hunched, his head outlined by a halo of light from his desk lamp, intent on filling cards with information he needed for his book on the history of the Jews in Poland. Sometimes he would make a note in pencil in the margin of a book: 'The evidence is inconclusive', or, 'This could be interpreted differently', or even, 'Here the author is definitely mistaken'. Sometimes he would incline his self-righteous, weary head and whisper to some tome on one of the shelves: 'This summer too will pass. Winter will come. And it is not going to be easy.' My mother would reply: 'Please don't say that.' Father: 'Why don't I get you a glass of tea. When you've drunk it, you must get some sleep. You're so tired.' There was a hesitancy in his voice, a midnight gentleness. In the hours of daylight he mostly spoke like a judge passing sentence.

One day a minor miracle occurred: one of Mr Lazarus's hens laid some eggs and sat on them till five chirping chicks hatched out. Even though we had never seen a cock. My mother made some joking remarks, but Father rebuked her:

'Stop it. The boy can hear.'

Mr Lazarus refused to sell the chicks. He gave each one a name. He spent the whole day pottering around on the sun-baked roof, with an expression of faint surprise, wearing a waistcoat, with a tape measure round his neck. He had hardly any work. Most of the time he argued in German with his hens, shouted at the chicks and forgave them, scattered seed, crooned lullabies, changed the sawdust, or stooped down and picked up a favourite chick, which he cradled against his breast and rocked like a baby.

Father said:

'If we have a little bread left over, or a cupful of soup –'

And my mother:

'I've sent him some already. The boy took it up, and some grits from yesterday too; we must go on saying it's for the chickens so as not to offend him. But what will happen in the long run?'

Father replied:

'We must do whatever we can, and hope.'

My mother said:

'There you go, talking like the wireless again. Stop it. The boy can hear.'

Every evening the three of us sat in the kitchen, after supper and the start of the curfew, playing Monopoly. My mother would clasp a glass of tea in her hands, absorbing its warmth even though it was summer. Or we would sort stamps and stick them in the album. Father liked to recount various facts about each country we came across. My mother soaked the stamps off the paper. After twenty minutes I fished the loosened stamps out of the basin of water and laid them out to dry on a sheet of blotting paper. The stamps lay there face downwards like the photograph of Italian prisoners of war captured by Field Marshal Montgomery in the Western Desert: they sat in rows on the burning sand, with their hands tied behind their backs and their faces hidden between their knees.

Then Father would identify the dried stamps with the help of the thick English catalogue that had on its cover an enlarged drawing of the stamp with a black swan, the most valuable stamp in the world even though its face value was only one penny. I would pass Father the transparent hinges on my outstretched hand, my eyes fixed on his lips. Father talked about some countries with polite loathing; others commanded his respect. He would talk about the population, the economy, the principal towns, the natural resources, the archaeological sites, the political regime, the artistic treasures. He always spoke especially about the great painters, musicians and poets who, by his account, were almost all Jews, or of Jewish descent, or at least half-Jews. Sometimes he would touch me on the head, or on the back, groping inside himself for some stifled affection, and suddenly he would say:

'Tomorrow you and I shall go to the newsagents. I'll buy you a pencil case. Or something else if you like. You're not happy enough.'

Once he said:

'I'm going to tell you something, a secret I've never told anybody. Please keep it just between the two of us. I'm a bit colour-blind. These things happen. It's a hereditary defect. It looks as though you'll have to see some things for the two of us. Yes indeed. After all, you are imaginative and intelligent.'

And there were words that Father used without realizing that they made Mother sad. Carpathians, for example. Or belfry. Also opera, carriage, ballet, cornice, clock square. (What is a cornice in fact? Or a gable? A weather vane? A porch? What

51

does a groom look like? Or a chancellor? A gendarme? A bell ringer?)

According to our fixed agreement my father or mother would come to my room at precisely ten-fifteen to make sure I had really turned my bedside light off. My mother would sometimes stay for five or ten minutes; she would sit on the edge of my bed and reminisce. Once she told me how, when she was a little girl of eight, she had sat one summer morning on the bank of a stream in the Ukraine, next to a flour mill. The water was dotted with ducks. She described the bend in the river where it disappeared into the forest. That was where things that the water carried away always disappeared: bark from trees or fallen leaves. In the yard of the mill she found a broken shutter painted pale blue and threw it into the stream. She had the impression that this stream, which came out of the forest and vanished into it again, had more bends inside the forest that completed the circle. So she sat there for two or maybe three hours, waiting for her shutter to complete the circuit and reappear. But only ducks came back.

At school she had been taught that water always flows downhill because such are the laws of nature and not otherwise. But surely in bygone times people believed in different natural laws; for instance they believed that the earth was flat and that the sun went round the earth and that the stars were put in the sky to watch over us. Maybe the natural laws of our own time were also temporary laws that would soon be replaced by new ones?

The next day she went back to the stream, but the blue shutter had not returned. On the days that followed she would sit and wait for half an hour or an hour on the bank of the stream, although she had worked out that the failure of the shutter to return proved nothing: the stream might well be circular, but the shutter might be stuck in the bank somewhere. Or in shallow water. Or it might already have floated past the mill, once or twice or even more often, but it could have happened at night, or at mealtimes, or perhaps it was while she was sitting waiting but at the precise moment it went past she had been looking up at a flight of birds and had missed it. Because large flocks of birds used to fly past in the autumn, the spring, even in summer, with no relation to the times of migration. In fact, how could you tell how big the circle was that the stream described before coming back to the mill? A week? A year? Maybe more? Perhaps at that very moment, when she was sitting on my bed telling me about the shutter, during the curfew in Jerusalem in nineteen forty-seven, the blue shutter from her childhood was still floating on the stream there, in the Ukraine, or in the valleys of the Carpathian Mountains, passing laundries, fountains, cornices and belfries. Still floating away from that flour mill, and who could say when it would reach its furthest point and start its return journey? It might take another ten years. Or seventy? Or a hundred and seven? Where was that blue shutter when my mother told me about it, more than twenty years after she threw it in? Where exactly were its remains? Its crumbled fragments? Its rotting debris? Surely there must have been something left then. And there must be something left even now, the evening I am writing this, some seventy years since the summer morning when my mother tossed it into the stream.

The day the shutter finally returns to the point where my mother threw it in the water, beneath the flour mill, it will not be seen by our eyes, for they will no longer exist, but by other eyes. The eyes of a man or woman who will be unable even to imagine that the object floating on the stream came from here and has now returned. What a pity, Mother said: if anyone sees my sign floating past the mill again, if they even notice it, how will they know that it is a sign, a proof that everything goes round in circles? In fact it is possible that the person who happens to be there on the very day and at the very moment when the shutter returns may also decide to make it a sign, to test whether or not the stream is circular. But, by the time it comes full circle again, that new person too will no longer exist. Another stranger will stand there and again won't have any idea. Hence the urge to tell.

13

MY TRIAL FOR treason in the Tel Arza Woods lasted less than a quarter of an hour, because we were afraid of being over-taken by the curfew. There was no interrogation under tor-ture and no barrage of insults. It was a cool and fairly polite trial. Chita Reznik opened it with the words:

'The accused will stand.' (A film starring Gary Cooper as a bandit sheriff from Montana had been showing at the Edison Cinema. My hearing was based on the lightning trial of the bandit sheriff.)

Ben Hur Tykocinski, the presiding judge, prosecutor, examining magistrate, sole witness and legislator, spoke with-out moving his lips:

'Proffy. Member of the High Command. Second-in-command and chief of operations. A central member of our organization. A capable man. Worthy of special approbation.'

I murmured:

'Thank you, Ben Hur.' (I was so proud I had a lump in my throat.)

Chita Reznik said:

'The accused will speak only when he is asked to do so. The accused will now be silent.'

Ben Hur answered him:

'Be quiet yourself Chita.'

After a moment's silence Ben Hur spoke a painful sentence with only three words:

'What a pity.'

He was silent again. Then, pensively, almost compassion-ately, he continued:

'We have three questions. The court will determine the punishment on the basis of the frankness of the answers to these questions. It will be very much to the accused's advantage to answer accurately. What was the motive? What did the enemy learn? And what was the reward of betrayal? The court will appreciate brief answers.'

I said:

'OK. It's like this. A: I'm not a traitor. On the contrary. I got important information out of the enemy under the guise of exchanging Hebrew and English lessons. That's . . . point A.'

Chita Reznik said:

'He's a liar. He's a low-down traitor and a liar.'

And Ben Hur:

'Chita. Final warning. Accused. Continue. Even briefer please.'

I continued:

'OK. B: I didn't inform. I didn't even give my name. And definitely not a hint about the existence of the Underground. Shall I go on?'

'If you're not too tired.'

Chita gave a nervous, servile laugh and said:

'Let me stew Proffy for a bit. Just five minutes. Then he'll sing like a canary.'

Ben Hur said:

'You're disgusting Chita. You're talking just like a little Nazi. Pick up that stone, little Nazi – no, that one there – and put it in your mouth. So. Now close your mouth. Now we'll have silence in court for the duration of the trial. The traitor will kindly conclude his speech, if he has not already done so.'

'C,' I said, forcing myself not to peep at Chita, who was almost choking on the stone. I was determined to stare firmly into those unblinking yellow fox-eyes. 'C: I received nothing from the enemy. Not a thread or a shoelace. As a matter of principle. I have finished. I wasn't a traitor, I was a spy. I followed my instructions precisely.'

'A touch overdone,' Ben Hur said sadly, 'with the thread and the shoelace and so on. But we're used to that. You spoke very well, Proffy.'

'Am I acquitted? Am I free?'

'The accused has finished. Now the accused will be quiet.'

There was another silence. Ben Hur Tykocinski stared at three little twigs. He tried four or five times to make them stand up like a tripod, but each time they collapsed. He pulled out his penknife, shortened one twig, whittled another, until he managed to stand them in a perfect geometrical arrangement. But he did not put the knife away, he balanced it on the back of his outstretched hand, with the blade pointing towards me, glinting. He said:

'This court believes the traitor when he says he got some information out of the enemy. This court even accepts that the traitor did not inform on us. The court rejects with disgust the traitor's false testimony that he did not receive any payment: the traitor received wafer biscuits, lemonade, a sausage roll, English lessons, and a Bible including the New Testament, which is a book attacking our people.'

'I didn't get a sausage roll,' I said almost in a whisper.

'The traitor is also petty. He is wasting the court's time with sausages and other irrelevant trifles.'

'Ben Hur!' A desperate sound suddenly burst out of me, an outcry of protest against injustice: 'What have I done to you? I didn't tell him anything. Not a word! And don't forget I set up this organization and made you commander-in-chief. But now that's all over. I hereby disband the FOD. The game is over. Have you ever heard of Dreyfus? Emile Zola, the writer? Of course not. But I don't care any more. This organization is disbanded and now I'm going home.'

'Go then, Proffy.'

'I'm going home, and I despise the two of you.'

'Go.'

'I'm not a traitor. I'm not an informer. It's all slander. As for you, Ben Hur, you're just a child with a persecution complex. I've got plenty of material about that in the encyclopedia.'

'Well? Why don't you go then? You keep saying you're going, you're going, and you're rooted to the spot. As for you, Chita, tell me, are you out of your mind? Stop eating stones. Yes. You can take it out. No, don't throw it away. Keep your stone, you might need it again.'

'What are you going to do to me?'

'You'll see, Proffy. It's not in the encyclopedia.'

Almost without a sound I said:

'But I didn't give anything away.'

'That's true.'

'And I didn't get anything from him.'

'That's more or less true, too. Or almost.'

'So why on earth?'

'Why. The traitor has read five encyclopedias and he still doesn't understand what he's done. Shall we explain to him? What do you think, Chita? Shall we open his eyes for him? Yes? Very well then. We're not Nazis. This court believes in issuing reasoned explanations of its decisions. Well then. It's because you love the enemy, Proffy. Loving the enemy, Proffy, is worse than betraying secrets. Worse than betraying fighters. Worse than informing. Worse than selling them arms. Even worse than going over and fighting on their side. Loving the enemy is the height of treachery. Come on, Chita. We'd better be going. Curfew will be starting soon. And it's unhealthy to breathe the same air as traitors. From now on, Chita, you're the second-in-command. Just keep your mouth shut.'

(Me? Stephen Dunlop? My whole stomach collapsed inwards, and everything in it was pushed down, down, a sensation like falling down a well. As if I had another stomach inside my stomach, a deep pit, and everything was pouring into it. Love? Him? It was a lie. The height of treachery? How could my mother say that anyone who loved wasn't a traitor?)

Ben Hur and Chita were a long way away. A roar exploded from me:

'You're crazy! You're mad! I hate that Dunlop, that medusa face! I hate him! I loathe him! I despise him!'

(Traitor. Liar. Low-down.)

Meanwhile, the woods were empty. The High Command had vanished. Soon it would be dark and the curfew would begin. I wouldn't go home. I'd go into the mountains and be a mountain boy. Live all on my own. For ever. Not belonging. And therefore not a traitor. Whoever belongs betrays.

Pine trees whispered and cypresses rustled: Shut up low-down traitor.

14

THESE WERE THE routes that were open to me, according to the logical plan that I had learned from my father to make in moments of crisis. I wrote them all down on a blank card taken from his desk. One: win Chita over to my side. (Stamps? Coins? Tell him a thriller in instalments?) And then vote Ben Hur out of his position as commander-in-chief. Two: split off. Found a new resistance movement and enlist new fighters. Three: run away to the Sanhedriya caves and live there until my innocence was clear. Or tell Sergeant Dunlop all about it, now that I had nothing more to lose. Ben Hur and Chita would go to prison and I would be taken off to England to start a new life under an entirely new identity. There, in England, I would forge links, make friends with government ministers and the King, until I found the right moment to strike at the heart of the regime and wrest our Land from them. Just me, on my own. And then I would grant Ben Hur and Chita a contemptuous amnesty.

Or not.

Better to wait.

I would gird myself with cast-iron patience and keep my eyes open. (I still give myself advice like this. I don't take it, though.)

I'll wait, calmly. If Ben Hur plots to harm me, I'll survive. But I won't take any steps that are liable to weaken or split the Underground. After their vengeance, after the punishment (and what more can they do to me?), they'll almost certainly ask me to rejoin them. Anyway, what can they do without me? They're just riffraff. Chickens with their heads cut off. But I won't be too quick to agree. I'll let them plead. Implore me. Beg my pardon. Acknowledge they did me an injustice.

'Dad,' I said that evening, 'what will we do if the British come along, say the High Commissioner or even the King himself, and acknowledge they have done us an injustice? And ask us to forgive them?'

My mother said:

'Of course we'll forgive them. How could we not? That's a lovely dream you've dreamed.'

'Albion,' said my father. 'First we'll have to examine carefully how sincere they are. Whether there's any ulterior motive. With them anything is possible.'

'How about if the Germans come and beg us to forgive them?'

'That's hard,' said my mother. 'That'll have to wait. Maybe in many years' time. Maybe you can do it. I can't.'

My father was deep in thought. Finally he touched me on the shoulder and said:

'So long as we Jews are few and weak, Albion and all the gentiles will go on sucking up to the Arabs. When we are very strong, when there are many of us and we can defend ourselves, yes indeed, then it is possible that they might come and speak sweetly to us. British, Germans, Russians, the whole world will come and serenade us. That day we will receive them politely. We will not reject their outstretched hands, but neither will we fall on their necks like long-lost brothers. On the contrary. Respect and suspect. By the way, it would be preferable for us to ally ourselves, not with the European nations, but with our Arab neighbours. After all, Ishmael is our only blood relative. Of course all this is a long way away, perhaps a very long way away. Do you remember the Trojan War? That we read together last winter? The well-known saying, "Beware the Greeks when they come bearing gifts"? Well, substitute British for Greeks. As for the Germans, so long as they do not forgive themselves, it is possible that one day we shall forgive them. But if it turns out that they do forgive themselves, we shall never forgive them.'

I didn't give up:

'But right at the end, will we forgive our enemies or not?'

(I had an image in my head at that moment, a precise, concrete, detailed image: Father and Mother and Sergeant Dunlop sitting together in this room on Saturday morning. Drinking tea and chatting in Hebrew about the Bible and archaeological sites in Jerusalem, arguing in Latin or classical Greek about Greeks bearing gifts. And Yardena and I were in a corner of the picture: she playing the clarinet and I lying on the rug not far from her feet, a happy panther in the basement.)

My mother said:

'Yes, we will. Not forgiving is like a poison.'

I ought to go and beg Yardena's pardon for what I nearly didn't see, not on purpose. For the thoughts that had come to me since then. But how could I? To beg her pardon I'd have to tell her what happened, and the story itself was a kind of betrayal. So that begging Yardena's pardon would be a kind of betrayal of a betrayal? Complicated. Does betrayal of a betrayal cancel out the original betrayal? Or does it make it twice as bad?

That's quite a question.

15

YOU MUST NEVER take a wounded Underground fighter to hospital, because that is the first place the CID will rush to after any operation, in search of injured fighters. That is why the Underground has its own secret dressing stations for taking care of the injured, and one of these was our apartment, because my mother studied nursing at the Hadassah Hospital when she first arrived in the country. (She studied for only two years, though, because in the second year she got married and in the third year I was born, thus cutting short her studies.)

There was a locked drawer in the bathroom cupboard. I was not allowed to ask what was in it or even to notice that it was always kept locked. But once, when my parents were at work, I carefully broke into it (with a bent piece of wire), and discovered a stock of bandages, dressings, syringes, various packets of pills, jars, sealed bottles, ointments with foreign writing on them. And I knew that if some night in the middle of the curfew I heard a furtive scraping at the door, followed by hushed voices, whispers, the scratch of a match on a matchbox, the whistling of the kettle, I was not to leave my room. Not to see the spare mattress spread out on the floor of the hallway under the big maps, which would have disappeared without trace by the morning. As though I had been dreaming. Not knowing is one of the hardest duties of an Underground man.

My father was almost blind in the dark, which is why he was never involved in night raids on barricades or fortified police stations. But he had a special task: it was to compose slogans in English denouncing Perfidious Albion, which had committed itself publicly to help us build a Jewish homeland here and was now, in an act of cynical betrayal, helping the Arabs to crush us. I asked my father what cynical betrayal meant. (Whenever Father explained a foreign idea to me he looked concentrated, responsible, like a scientist pouring a precious fluid from one test tube to another.) He said:

'Cynical: cold and calculated. Selfish. The word comes from *kyon*, the ancient Greek word for a dog. When a suitable opportunity presents itself I shall explain to you the connection between cynicism and dogs, which ironically enough are normally considered to symbolize loyalty. It is rather a long story, testifying to the ingratitude of men towards those animals that are most useful to them, such as the dog, the mule, the horse, the donkey, which have become terms of abuse, whereas dangerous wild beasts, such as the lion, the tiger, the wolf and even the scavenging vulture, receive undeserved respect in most languages. Anyway, to come back to your question, cynical betrayal is cold-blooded, immoral and unfeeling betrayal.'

I asked (myself, not Father): Is there any betrayal that is not cynical? That is not selfish and calculated. Is there such a thing as a traitor who is not low-down? (Today I think there is.)

In Father's English slogans for the Underground, Perfidious Albion was accused of continuing the crimes of the Nazis, of selling the last hopes of a decimated nation for Arab oil and military bases in the Middle East.

'The people of Milton and Lord Byron should realize that the oil that warms them in winter is stained with the spilled blood of the survivors of the persecuted people.' 'The British Labour Government is sucking up to corrupt Arab regimes that are constantly moaning that they don't have enough room between the Atlantic Ocean and the Persian Gulf and from Mount Ararat in the north to Bab al-Mandab in the deepest south.' (I checked on the map: they were really not short of space. Our land was a tiny dot in the vast expanse of the Arab world, a pinhead in the British Empire.) When we finished building our rocket, we would aim it at the King's palace in the heart of London, and force them to get out of our land. (And what would happen to Sergeant Dunlop? He loved the Bible and us. Would he get permission to stay here, as a special honoured guest of the Hebrew State? I'd make sure of it. I'd write a reference for him.)

Father wrote his slogans at night, when he wasn't researching the history of the Jews in Poland. He quoted lines of English poetry in them, to stir their hearts. In the morning on his way to work he handed the sheet of paper, concealed inside his newspaper, to his contact man (the boy who looked like a stork and helped in the Sinopsky Brothers grocery). The slogans were then taken to the secret printing press (in the Kolodnys' cellar). A couple of days later they appeared on walls of buildings, on lampposts, and even on the walls of the police station where Sergeant Dunlop was based.

If the CID discovered Mother's locked drawer or the drafts of Father's slogans, the two of them would be imprisoned in the Russian Compound, and I would be left on my own. I would go away to the mountains and live the life of a mountain boy.

I saw a film at the Edison Cinema about a gang of counterfeiters: a whole family, brothers, cousins, and in-laws. When I got home, I asked Mother if we were also a family of outlaws. She said:

'What have we done? Have we robbed anybody? Have we cheated anybody? Have we shed anybody's blood, heaven forbid?'

And Father:

'Certainly not. On the contrary: British law is actually illegal. Their very rule here rests on repression and falsehood, because they were given Jerusalem by the nations of the world on the basis of their commitment to establish a Jewish national home, and now they are urging the Arabs on to destroy this home and even helping them to do it.' As he spoke, anger blazed in his blue eyes which were magnified by the lenses of his glasses. My mother and I exchanged covert glances, because Father's anger was a gentle, literary anger. Driving out the British and repelling the Arab armies required a different sort of anger, a savage anger far from words, a kind of anger that did not exist in our homes or in our neighbourhood. Maybe it existed only in Galilee, in the valleys, in the kibbutzim in the Negev, in the mountains where every night the fighters of the real Underground trained. Maybe in those places the right sort of anger was building up. We didn't know what that anger was like, but we did know that without it we were all doomed. Out there, in the desert, in the plain, on the Carmel range, in the burning valley of Beit Shean, a new breed of Jews was growing up, who were not pale and bespectacled like us but bronzed and strong, they were pioneers, and they had wellsprings of the real, murderous kind of anger. The indignant anger that occasionally flashed from Father's glasses made Mother and me smile imperceptibly. Less than a wink. A mini-conspiracy, an Underground within the Underground, as though for an instant she had opened a forbidden drawer in my presence. As though she was hinting to me that there were certainly two adults and a child in the room, but that in her mind at least I was not necessarily the child. Not all the time, anyway. I suddenly went over and hugged her hard while Father was switching on his desk lamp and sitting down to go on gathering facts for his history of the Jews in Poland. So why was the sweetness of that moment mingled with the sour sense of squeaking chalk, the dull taste of treachery?

At that moment I made up my mind to tell them:

'I've finished with Ben Hur and Chita. We're not friends any more.'

Father had his back to us and his face to the piles of books that lay open on his desk. He asked:

'What have you done now? When will you learn to be loyal to your friends?'

I said:

'We've had a split.'

Father turned in his chair and inquired in his self-righteous voice: 'A split? Between the Sons of Light and the Sons of Darkness?'

And Mother:

'They're shooting out there in the dark again. It sounds quite close.'

16

I HAVE ALREADY MENTIONED how fascinated I am by people like Ben Hur, people who are always thirsty, whose unquenchable thirst gives them the drowsy cruelty of a wild cat – cool authority with half-closed eyes. And like the heroes of King David we studied in Bible class, I always feel a strange urge to put everything I have on the line for them. To risk my life fetching them water from enemy wells. All in the vague hope of hearing afterwards from the corner of the leopard's mouth the magical words: 'You're OK, Proffy.'

There is another kind of people who enthrall me, apart from those thirsty leopards. On the face of it these people are the diametrical opposite of the leopards, but actually they do have something in common that is impossible to define but not hard to spot. I mean people who are always lost. Like Sergeant Dunlop, for instance. Both at the time I am writing about and now as I write, I have always found something poignantly endearing about lost people, who go through life as though the world is a strange bus station in an unfamiliar city, where they have alighted by mistake and now have no idea where they went wrong or how to get out, or where to.

He was fairly broad and tall, a large pudgy man, but he was gentle. Rather cartilaginous. Despite his uniform and his gun, the sergeant's stripes on his sleeves, the glint of silvery numbers on his shoulders, the black peaked cap, he looked like a man who has just come out of the light into the dark, or out of darkness into bright light.

He looked like a man who once lost something very

precious, and now he can't remember what it was he lost, what it looks like, or what he would do with it if he found it. So there he was, always wandering in his own inner chambers, in the corridors, in the basement, in the storerooms, and even if he stumbled on whatever it was he had lost, how would he recognize it? He would walk wearily past and keep on searching. He would plod onwards in his big boots getting ever further away and more and more lost. I did not forget that he represented the enemy, and yet I had a kind of urge to hold out a hand to him. Not to shake hands, but to support him. Like a baby, or a blind man.

Almost every evening I used to slink into the Orient Palace, with copies of *English for Overseas Students* and *Our Language for Immigrant and Pioneer* under my arm. I no longer cared if the leopard and his sidekick were still trailing me along the alleys.

What more did I have to lose?

I quickly crossed the decadent front room, with its cigarette smoke and its stench of beer, ignoring the ribald laughter, restraining the urge of my fingertips to stroke the green baize of the billiard table, not seeing the barmaid's cleavage; in a straight line, with the determination of an arrow in flight, I sped into the back room and landed beside his table.

More than once it turned out that I had come in vain: he was not there, even though we had made an arrangement. Sometimes he forgot. Sometimes he had got muddled. Sometimes when he finished his day's work in the accounts department he was suddenly sent on some outdoor assignment, standing guard on the post office or checking identity cards at a roadblock. And occasionally, so he hinted to me, he was confined to barracks because he had been slow in saluting or because one of his boots was shinier than the other.

Who has ever seen, in real life or in a film, a scatterbrained enemy? Or a shy one? Sergeant Dunlop was a scatterbrained and very shy enemy. Once, I asked him if he had a wife or children waiting for him back home in Canterbury. (This was intended as an inoffensive way of hinting to him that the time had definitely come for the British to get out of our land, for their own good as well as ours.) Sergeant Dunlop was alarmed by my question, his heavy head withdrew into his shoulders like a startled tortoise, his big freckled hands scampering in confusion from his knees to the tabletop and back again, and then he turned red from his cheeks to his forehead and ears, like a wine stain spreading on a white tablecloth. He embarked on a lengthy apology in his rococo Hebrew: for the time being he 'walked his path in solitude', even though the Good Lord had told us specifically in the Good Book that 'it is not good for the man to be alone'.

Sometimes I found Sergeant Dunlop sitting waiting for me at his usual table, his shirttails hanging out of his trousers, his belly flopping over his belt and obscuring its shiny buckle – a slack, fleshy man. He might be playing himself at draughts, and on my arrival he would give a little start, apologize, and hurriedly put the pieces away in the box. He would say something like:

'Either way, I shall soon lose.' And he would smile a sort of please-don't-take-any-notice-of-me smile, and halfway through smiling he would blush, and it seemed as though the blushing increased his embarrassment, and so redoubled itself.

'On the contrary,' I said to him once, 'either way, you will win.'

He thought about this, got the point, and smiled sweetly, as though I had uttered a remark that was beyond the wisest philosopher. After thinking it over again he replied:

'Not so. In my victory I shall defeat myself.'

Nevertheless, he agreed to play me just once, and won, which filled him with rueful embarrassment. He started to apologize as though by beating me he had personally added to the crimes of the oppressive British regime.

Sometimes in the course of my English lessons he would apologize for the complicated tense system and the large number of irregular verbs. He seemed to be blaming himself and his sloppiness for the fact that English so often makes do with one word where Hebrew has two: for instance one speaks of 'a glass of water' and 'a pane of glass'; 'a dining table' and 'a statistical table'; 'a grizzly bear' and 'to bear a burden'; 'a hot day' and 'a hot curry'; 'to make a date' and 'to

67

eat a date'. Whereas in his own Hebrew lessons, whenever he handed in the homework I set him, he would ask humbly:

'Well? A brutish man knoweth not? Neither doth a fool understand?'

If I praised his work, his childlike eyes would light up, and a modest, heartwarming smile would tremble on his lips before overflowing to his round cheeks; it seemed to spread all over his body under his uniform. He would murmur:

'I am not worthy of this praise.'

But sometimes, right in the middle of a lesson, we would put our business on one side and talk. Sometimes he would get carried away and tell me all the barrack-room gossip, chuckling as though he was shocked by the naughtiness that was coming out of his mouth: who was undermining whose authority, who was hoarding sweets or cigarettes, who never took a bath, who had been seen drinking in the bar with someone he claimed was his sister.

If we discussed the political situation, I became an angry prophet and he merely nodded and said 'Indeed' or 'Woe'. Once he said:

'The people of the Prophets. The people of the Book. If only they could come to their inheritance without shedding innocent blood.'

Sometimes the conversation turned to the Biblical stories, and then it was my turn to listen open-mouthed while he amazed me with observations that our teacher Mr Zerubbabel Gihon could not have contemplated in his wildest dreams. It emerged, for instance, that Sergeant Dunlop did not like King David, even though he felt sorry for him. His David was a village boy who was cut out to be a poet and a lover, but God made him king, which did not suit him, and condemned him to living a life of wars and intrigues. Small wonder that at the end of his life David was tormented by the same evil spirit that he himself had inflicted on his predecessor, Saul, who was a better man than he. In the end the two of them, the ass driver and the shepherd, suffered the same fate.

Sergeant Dunlop talked about Saul and David and Michal and Jonathan and Absalom and Joab in tones of faint wonderment, as if they, too, were youngsters from the Hebrew Underground whom he had once sat with in the Orient Palace, learning Hebrew from them and teaching them a little Philistine in return. He felt affection and compassion for Saul and Jonathan, but he was fondest of all of Saul's daughter Michal, who never had a child, and he also liked Paltiel son of Laish, who wept for her until Avner banished him and so, pursuing yet not pursuing the wife who was no longer his, he too was banished from the stage and disappeared from the chronicle.

But apart from Paltiel, I thought to myself, almost all of them were traitors: Jonathan and Michal betrayed their father Saul; Joab and the other sons of Zeruiah, the fair Absalom, Amnon, Adonijah son of Hagith – they were all traitors, and the worst traitor of all was King David himself, David about whom we sing the song, 'David King of Israel lives, lives, lives on still'. They all seemed faintly comical in Sergeant Dunlop's version: miserable fusspots who seemed rather like the CID officers that he told me snippets of gossip about: one was jealous, another obsequious, a third suspicious. In his stories they all seemed trapped in a surreal web of infatuations, desires, jealousies and intrigues, and the pursuit of power and vengeance. (Here they are again, those thirsty men, those parched leopards whose thirst no water in the world can quench, ever. Pursuing and pursued. Blind men, digging a pit and falling into it.)

I looked in vain for a crushing reply that would rescue the honour of King David and Mr Gihon – and in fact the honour of our whole people. I knew that it was my duty in these conversations to defend something or other from whatever Sergeant Dunlop was doing to it. But what was it I was supposed to defend? I did not know then (and I don't fully know today). And yet my heart went out to them all, to Saul, abandoned and deceived, tried by Samuel for betrayal and condemned to paying with his crown and his life for not having a heart of stone. To Michal and Jonathan, whose souls were so bound to the soul of the enemy of their family that they did not hesitate to betray their father and his throne and to follow the leopard. I even felt kindly towards David, the traitor-king who betrayed all those who loved him and was betrayed by almost all of them in turn.

Why couldn't we all get together just once in the back room of the Orient Palace, Sergeant Dunlop, Mother, Father, Ben Gurion, Ben Hur, Yardena, the Grand Mufti Haj Amin, my teacher Mr Gihon, the leaders of the Underground, Mr Lazarus and the High Commissioner, all of us, even Chita and his mother and his two alternate fathers, and chat for an hour or two, and understand each other at last, make some concessions, be reconciled, and forgive one another? Why couldn't we all go down to the bank of the stream together to see if the blue shutter had been carried back yet?

'That is enough for today,' Sergeant Dunlop would cut through my dreams. 'Let us part now and return tomorrow: in the sweat of our brow we shall increase knowledge, oh that we might not also increase sorrow.'

Whereupon we would part, without shaking hands, because he had understood of his own accord that I was forbidden to shake hands with the foreign oppressor. So we made do with a nod of the head on meeting and parting.

And what was the secret information that I managed to get out of Sergeant Dunlop as a result of our relationship?

Not much; just a tidbit here and there.

Something about the sleeping arrangements in the fortified police station.

Something (quite important actually) about the night duty rosters.

Personal relations among the officers and among their wives. Some details about barracks routine.

And something else that cannot perhaps be seen as the result of my spying, but which I shall mention here anyway. On one occasion Sergeant Dunlop said to me that in his opinion after the end of the British Mandate a Hebrew State would be set up here and the words of the Prophets would come true exactly as recorded in the Bible, and yet he felt sorry for the peoples of Canaan, by which he meant the local Arabs, and particularly for the villagers. He believed that after the British army had left, the Jews would arise and defeat their enemies, the stone-built villages would be destroyed, the fields and gardens would be turned into haunts of jackals and foxes, the wells would dry up, and the peasants and farmers and olive pickers, the dressers of sycamore trees and shepherds and drivers of she-asses would all be driven out into the wilderness. Perhaps it was the Creator's decree that they should become a persecuted people, instead of the Jews, who were returning at long last to their inheritance. 'Wonderful are the ways of the Lord,' Sergeant Dunlop said sadly and with an air of faint astonishment, as though he had suddenly reached a conclusion that had been long awaiting him: 'the one he loves he chastizes, and the one he would uproot he loves.'

17

A RUMOUR RAN ROUND the neighbourhood: the British were
about to impose a general, day and night, curfew and to con-
duct extensive house-to-house searches to uncover Underground fighters and caches of arms.

When Father came home from work that afternoon he
called the three of us together for a short meeting in the
kitchen. There was something we had to discuss seriously and
frankly. He closed the door and the window, sat down in his
well-pressed khaki clothes with their wide pockets, and
placed a small package wrapped in brown paper on the table
in front of him. There was something inside it, he said, or
strictly speaking some things, that we had been asked to hide
until the troubles were over. It was certainly reasonable to
suppose that the searches would not pass us by, but it was
believed that it was easier to find a hiding place for this thing,
or these things, in our apartment. And we were definitely prepared to stand the test.

I thought: He's right not to tell us what's in the package, so
as not to alarm Mother. (What if he doesn't know himself?
That's not possible: Father does know.) As for me, I immediately assumed that it contained dynamite or TNT or nitro-
glycerine or something much stronger, some new-found,
revolutionary explosive substance the like of which had never
been seen before: some doomsday compound that we had
developed here in secret Underground laboratories. A spoon-
ful of it could blow up half the city.

What about me?

Half a teaspoonful would be enough for our rocket that would threaten the King's palace in London.

This was the moment of opportunity I had been waiting for. I must at all costs secretly extract from the package the quantity I needed.

If I succeeded, the FOD would get down on its knees to plead with me to forgive them and come back.

And I would forgive them. Contemptuously. And agree to come back. But I would have to secure a few serious concessions: to reorganize the command from scratch, put Ben Hur in his place, abolish the department of Internal Security and Interrogation, and find a way of preventing arbitrary decisions and protect fighters from the dangers of internal malice.

Father said:

'If and when we are searched, it is essential that you two should know what it is about, for two reasons: first, there's not much room here and somebody might find it by accident and cause an incident. Second, if they do find the hiding place they may question us separately, and I want us all to have an identical explanation ready. Not to contradict each other.' (The explanation that Father asked us to memorize had to do with Professor Schlossberg, who had lived alone on the floor above ours and died the previous winter. He left Father fifty or sixty books in his will. Our unanimous reply to questioning was to be that the brown paper parcel came into our apartment with the late professor's books.)

'It will be a white lie,' Father said, and his shortsighted blue eyes looked through his spectacle frames straight into my own eyes. For an instant a rare, mischievous glint shone in his eye, such as I had seen only very occasionally, when he recounted how he had delivered a crushing reply to some scholar or writer, who had been left 'speechless, as though thunderstruck'. 'We shall permit ourselves to use this white lie in case of need, only because of the danger, and we shall do it with regret, because a lie is a lie. Always. Even a white lie is still a lie. Kindly take note of that.'

Mother said:

'Instead of lecturing him, why don't you find time to play

with him once in a while? Or at least talk to him? A conversation: do you remember? Two people sit down together, they both talk and they both listen? Both trying to follow what the other is saying?'

Father picked up the package, cradled it in his arms like a crying baby, and carried it from the kitchen to the room that served as my parents' bedroom, my father's study and a living room for all of us. The walls were lined with bookshelves from floor to ceiling. There was not space for a single picture or ornament.

Father's bookshelves were organized with an iron logic into sections and subsections, by subject and field and language, and alphabetically by author's name. The top brass, the field marshals and generals of the library, that is the special tomes that always gave me a thrill of respect, were priceless, heavy books clad in splendid leather bindings. On their rough leather surface my fingers sought out the delightful impression of the golden lettering, like the chest of some field marshal in the Fox Movietone newsreels bedecked with rows and rows of gleaming medals and decorations. When a single ray of light from Father's desk lamp fell on their ornate gold ornamentation, a flickering sparkle leaped towards my eyes, seeming to invite me to join them. These books were my princes, dukes, earls, and barons.

Above them, on the shelf just below the ceiling, hovered the light cavalry: periodicals in many-coloured wrappers, arranged by topic, date and country of origin. In striking contrast to the heavy armour of the commanding officers, these cavalrymen were dressed in light robes of exciting colours.

Around the cluster of field marshals and generals stood large clumps of brigade and regimental officers, rough, tough-shouldered books, in strong cloth bindings, dusty, slightly faded, as though dressed in sweaty, grubby camouflage battle dress, or like the fabric of old flags, tested in battle and hardship.

Some of the books showed a narrow gap between their cloth binding and their bodies, like the cleavage of the barmaid in the Orient Palace. If I peeped inside I could see only a fragrant darkness, and catch a faint echo of the scent of the

74

book's body, vague, fascinating and forbidden.

Ranking lower than the officer books in their cloth bindings were the hundreds and hundreds of simple books bound in rough cardboard, smelling of cheap glue – the grey and brown privates of the library. Even lower than these privates in my estimation were the rabble of semi-regular militias: unbound books whose pages were held together by tired rubber bands or wide strips of sticky paper. There were also some shabby gangs of bandits, in disintegrating yellowish paper wrappers. Finally, beneath these, were the lowest of the low, the non-books, a mixed multitude of mendicant leaflets, offprints, handbills, on the lowest rung of the bookcase – flotsam and jetsam huddled on the bottommost shelf, waiting for Father to remove them to some asylum for unwanted publications, and meanwhile here they were, temporarily camped, out of kindness not of right, heaped up, crowded together, until today or tomorrow the east wind with the birds of the desert would sweep their corpses away, until today or tomorrow, or at the latest by the winter, Father would find the time to sort them out ruthlessly and throw most of these charity cases (brochures, gazettes, magazines, journals, pamphlets) out of the apartment, to make room for other beggars, whose day would not be slow to arrive. (Father took pity on them, however. Again and again he promised himself to sort them, make a selection, get rid of some, but I had the feeling that not a single printed page ever left our apartment, although it was bursting at the seams.)

A fine, dusty smell hovered around these bookcases, like the deposit left by a turbulent, yet exciting, foreign air. To this day you can take me to a room, even with my eyes closed and my ears plugged, and I can always tell at once, without the slightest doubt, if it is a room full of books. I take in the smells of an old library not with my nostrils but through my skin, a kind of grave, pensive place laden with a book dust finer than any other dust, blended with the savour that emanates from old paper, mingled with the smell of glues ancient and modern, pungent thick almond scents, sourish sweat, intoxicating alcohol-based adhesives, a distant whiff of the world of sea-weed and iodine, and undertones of the lead smell of thick printer's ink, and a smell of rotting paper, eaten away by damp and mildew, and of cheap paper that is crumbling to dust, contrasting with the rich, exotic, dizzying aromas emanating from fine imported art paper that excite the palate. The whole overlaid with a covering of dark air that has been fixed motionless for year upon year, caught in the secret spaces between the rows of books and the wall behind them.

In the wide, heavy bookcase to the left of Father's desk the bulky reference works were assembled, like the supporting artillery dug in to the rear of the storm troops: row upon row of multi-volume encyclopedias in various languages, dictionaries, a gigantic biblical concordance, an atlas, lexicons and handbooks (including one book entitled *Index of Indexes*, in which I hoped to find deep secrets but which actually contained nothing but lists of thousands of books with weird names). The encyclopedias, dictionaries, and lexicons were nearly all field marshals and generals, that is to say splendid leather-bound tomes with gold writing that my fingertips longed to stroke and fondle, that fascinated me not only with the delight of touching them but also with longing for the endless expanse of knowledge that was beyond my reach because it was in foreign languages – knowledge about things like the cross, the hussar, the steeple, the forest, the cottage and the meadow, the carriage and the streetcar, the cornice, porch, and gable. And what am I in comparison? Nothing but a young Hebrew Underground fighter, whose life is devoted to driving out the foreign oppressor but whose soul is bound up with his because the oppressor, too, comes from lands with rivers and forests, where belfries stand forth proudly and weather-vanes rotate sedately on the roof.

Around the golden letters that were stamped on the leather bindings were decorative flowers and sprigs, emblems of the publishing house or library, which seemed to me like the arms and blazons of so many royal and noble houses. There were even winged dragons and pairs of furious golden lions supporting a closed or unrolled scroll, or an impression of a castle, or twisted crosses like the piercing crooked serpent we learned about in Bible class.

Occasionally Father would lay his hand on my shoulder

and invite me on a guided tour. This is the rare Amsterdam edition. The Talmud printed by the widow and brothers Romm. These are the arms of the Kingdom of Bohemia that no longer exists. This binding is made of deerskin, which is why it is pinkish, the colour of raw flesh. And here we have a priceless edition of the Year of the Creation 5493 (corresponding to the civil year 1733), perhaps from the library of the great Moses Hayyim Luzzatto, who may even have handled it himself. It has no equal, even in the rare books collection in the National Library on Mount Scopus, and, who knows, there may be only another dozen copies left in the whole world, or even seven or fewer. (Father's words made me think of Abraham bargaining with God about the number of righteous men in Sodom.)

From here to here is Greek. On the shelf above, Latin, the language of ancient Rome. Over there, all along the north wall, extends the Slavic world, whose very alphabet is a mystery to me. Here are the French and Spanish sections, and on the shelf over there, looking dark and serious as though in formal dress, the representatives of the Germanic world whisper together in their own corner. (Complicated curly letters, 'Gothic letters' Father said, without elaborating, and this Gothic script seemed to me like a sinister labyrinthine maze of intersecting paths.) While over there, in a glass-fronted bookcase, crowd the assembled texts of our forefathers (never foremothers: forefathers, before-fathers, ancient ghosts): the Mishnah, the two Talmuds, the Babylonian and the Jerusalemite, law and lore, hymns and angelologies, Mekhilta and Zohar, novellae and responsa, glossaries and grammars, *Teacher of Knowledge* and *Stone of Help*, *Path of Life* and *Breastplate of Judgment*, fables, lives of the saints, constituting a kind of dark suburb, a strange, gloomy landscape like a huddle of miserable hovels lit by a faint lantern, and yet they were not entirely foreign to me, these distant relations, because even bizarre titles like *Tosefta*, *Spread Table*, *Yosippon* or *The Duties of the Hearts* were inscribed in Hebrew characters that gave me at least some right to speculate about what was spread on the Spread Table or what were the duties that lay upon those Hearts.

77

Then came the history sections: four cramped bookcases, in one of which some refugee tomes were squeezed, latecomers who had found no resting place and had to make do by reclining precariously on the shoulders of their longer-established predecessors. Two of these four cases were devoted to the history of the nations and two to that of the Jewish people. In the former I found on the bottom shelf the dawn of mankind, the beginning of civilization, and on the next shelf up ancient history, and then the Middle Ages (blood-chilling drawings, dark-robed doctors in devilish masks bending over dying victims of the Black Death). Above these, in bright daylight, the Renaissance and the French Revolution, and higher still, so high they were almost touching the ceiling, were books about the October Revolution and the World Wars, which I strove to study in order to learn a lesson from an examination of the mistakes of earlier generals. Those books that I could not read because they were in foreign languages I nevertheless scanned page by page in tireless search of illustrations and maps. Many of these are engraved on my memory to this day: The Exodus from Egypt. The Collapse of the Walls of Jericho. The Battle of Thermopylae: dense forests of lances, javelins, spears, and helmets reflecting the flashing sunlight. The map of the travels of Alexander the Great, with bold arrows extending from the borders of Greece to Persia and even to India. And a picture of heretics being burned in a town square, showing the flames already licking at their feet, and yet their eyes are closed in piety and spiritual concentration, as though they can hear at last the celestial music. And the expulsion of the Jews from Spain: masses of refugees bearing parcels and sticks crowded together in a decrepit ship on a stormy sea seething with monsters that seem happy about the fate of the banished Jews. Or a detailed plan of the eastern Diaspora, with thick circles around Salonica, Smyrna, and Alexandria. A vivid colour picture of an old synagogue in Aleppo. And faraway communities of scattered Jews sprouting at the edges of the map, in Yemen, Cochin, Ethiopia (which was called Abyssinia at that time). And a picture of Napoleon at Moscow, and Napoleon again in Cairo at the foot of the pyramids: a small, portly man with a three-cornered hat on his head, one hand pointing boldly towards the vast expanse of the horizon, the other concealed coyly inside his coat. The wars of the Hasidim and their opponents: portraits of grim-faced rabbis. A detailed map of the spread of the Hasidic courts and the receding lines of defence behind which the retreating Mitnagdim entrenched themselves without abandoning their opposition. And stories of exploration and discovery, with fleets of sailing ships whose carved prows pass through straits in unknown archipelagoes, of inaccessible continents, empires, the Wall of China, Japanese palaces that no man could enter and live, and savage inhabitants dressed in feathers, with bones stuck through their noses. And maps of the whale hunters, the polar sea, and the Bering Sea, with Alaska and the Gulf of Murmansk. And here is Theodor Herzl leaning on an iron railing and staring proudly and dreamily towards the lake that stretches at his feet. Immediately after Herzl, the first pioneers appear, few and miserable, huddled like abandoned sheep in a desolate landscape consisting of nothing but sand and a solitary olive tree, slightly to one side. And a map of the early Jewish settlement: a few scattered acres, spreading from map to map and strengthening from table to table. And here is Comrade Lenin, in a cap, making a speech, firing with enthusiasm the crowds who are waving clenched fists. This Lenin looks to me a bit like our own Dr Weitzman, who never stops pleading with the British instead of hitting at them. (How about Sergeant Dunlop? Should we hit at him, too?) And here is a map of the Nazi camps, with photographs of skeletal Jewish survivors. And here are plans of famous battles, Tobruk, Stalingrad, Sicily, and here at last marches the Jewish Brigade, Hebrew warriors with the six-pointed star on their sleeves, in Africa and Italy, and pictures of tower-and-stockade kibbutzim in the hills, in the desert, in the valleys, intrepid pioneers mounted on horses or tractors, with rifles slung aslant their chests, their faces calm and courageous.

I would shut the book and replace it in its correct spot, then I would take down another, and again turn the pages, searching, particularly for illustrations and maps. By the end of an hour or two I was slightly intoxicated, a panther in the basement, bursting with oaths and vows, clearly aware of what I had to do and what I had to devote my life to, and for what, when the moment of truth came, I had to sacrifice it.

At the front of the big German atlas, even before the map of Europe, came a dizzying map of the whole universe, with nebulas extending away beyond the bounds of the imagination and endless expanses of unfamiliar stars. Father's library resembled that map. It contained familiar planets, but it also had its mysterious nebulas, Lithuanian and Latin, Ukrainian and Slovak, and even a very ancient language named Sanskrit. And there was Aramaic, and there was Yiddish, which was a kind of satellite of Hebrew, a craggy, pitted orb floating wanly over our heads, among the tattered clouds. And light-years away from Yiddish there were more and more firmaments, where the Epic of Gilgamesh twinkled remotely, and Enuma Elish, and the Homeric Hymns and Siddhartha, and wonderful poems called, for example, *Nibelungenlied*, *Hiawatha*, *Kalevala*. Musical names that thrill the tip of my tongue and my palate when I roll them around in my mouth and pronounce them inwardly, in a whisper, only to myself, Dante Alighieri, Montesquieu, Chaucer, Shchedrin, Aristophanes, Till Eulenspiegel. And I recognize each one by its colour and binding and its place in its own galaxy, and know who its neighbours are.

And what about me? Who am I within this great universe? A blind panther. An ignorant savage. A scamp who spends his time messing around in the Tel Arza woods. A wretched plaything in the hands of some wretched Ben Hur. Instead of shutting myself up at once, from today, from this morning, here among these books.

For ten years?

For thirty?

Breathing deeply, plunging into the well, starting to crack one riddle after another?

What a long journey, how many bewildering secrets are contained within these tomes whose very names I can just about decipher. I cannot even imagine where to find the first link in the keychain attached to the key of the casket containing the key to the safe in which the key to the outermost court of all may perhaps be waiting for me.

First of all I must overcome the difficulty of the Roman alphabet. Mother said she could teach it to me in less than half an hour. After that, if I helped her with the washing up after supper, she promised to teach me the Cyrillic alphabet. She reckoned that could be done in an hour or an hour and a half. As for Father, he promised that the Greek alphabet was very similar to the Cyrillic.

After that I would learn Sanskrit, too.

And I would learn another dialect, that Father called *Hochdeutsch*, which he translated as 'High German'.

The name High German had a flavour of bygone times, of walled towns with wooden drawbridges guarded by twin turrets capped by conical roofs. Within the walls of these towns lived austere scholars with black robes and bare heads, who sat night after night reading and studying and writing by the light of a candle or oil lamp in a cell whose only window was barred. I would be like them: cell, lattice, candle at night, desk, pile of books, and silence.

The bookshelves reduced the size of the room considerably. And it was not a large room to start with. Here, below the ranks of books, was my parents' bed. At night they opened it up to sleep in, and in the morning they closed it like a book, with the mattress inside, thus turning it into a green-covered sofa. There were five embroidered cushions on it, which I used for the five hills of Rome when I led the forces of Bar Kochba to the foot of the Capitol and subdued the Empire. Another time they represented the hills commanding the road to the Negev, or white whales that I pursued across the Seven Seas to the shores of Antarctica.

Between the sofa bed and Father's desk, between the desk and the coffee table and the two wicker stools, and between them and Mother's rocking chair, there were canals or straits, all coming together at the little rug at the foot of the rocking chair. This arrangement of furniture afforded me fascinating opportunities to deploy columns of ships or land armies, enacting breakouts, outflanking movements, assaults, ambushes, and stubborn resistance in densely built-up areas.

Father put the package in a place that he had cleverly

selected, in the middle of a row of uniform editions of gems of world literature in Polish translation. This series had a light-brown binding, so that the parcel blended in and almost disappeared among the books. Like a real dragon in a dense tropical forest full of gigantic trees that all looked like dragons. He repeated his warning to me and Mother: Don't touch. Don't go near it. The whole library was henceforth out of bounds. If anyone needed a book, would they kindly address themselves to him. (I found this insulting. Admittedly Mother might make a mistake or forget what she was doing while dusting, but what about me? I knew the whole library by heart. I could locate every section, district, and cranny blindfold. I could find my way around almost as well as Father himself. Like a young panther in the jungle he was born and raised in.) I decided not to remonstrate: by eight o'clock tomorrow morning they would both be out of the apartment and I would be the High Commissioner of this whole kingdom. Including the place of the dragon. Including the dragon itself.

18

NEXT MORNING, THE instant the door closed behind them, I approached the shelf and stood a breath's space away, without touching. I tried to make out whether the package was exhaling a faint chemical smell, at least a whiff of a smell? But only the smells of the library, civilian smells of glue dust and bygone days, surrounded me. I went back to the kitchen to tidy away the remains of breakfast. I washed the dishes and laid them out to drain. I went from room to room closing the shutters and windows against the incursions of summer. Then I started to patrol the route between the front door and the hiding place, backwards and forwards, a panther in a basement. I was utterly unable to return to the plans for the attack on Government House that I had been busy with until yesterday. That brown package, disguised as a literary gem in Polish, slumbering innocently on the shelf, fascinated me like a kind of Pandora's box.

At first the temptations were weak and coy, hardly daring to hint to me what I really wanted. But gradually they became bolder, more explicit, licking at the toes of my sandals, tickling the palms of my hands, calling out to me brazenly, pulling me shamelessly by the sleeve.

Temptations are like sneezes, which start from nothing at all, a faint pinching sensation at the base of your nose, and then gradually take over so that there's no stopping them. Temptations generally start from a little patrol to check the terrain, tiny ripples of vague, undefined excitement, and, before you know what it wants of you, you start to feel a

83

gradual glow inside, like when you switch on an electric fire and the element is still grey but it starts to make little popping noises and then it blushes very faintly and then more deeply and soon it is glowing angrily and you are full of reckless lightheadedness; so what, what the hell, why not, what harm can it do, like a very vague but wild, uninhibited sound deep inside you, coaxing and pleading with you: come on, why not, just put the tip of your finger very close to the wrapping paper on the secret package, just feel it without touching, just sense with the pores of your skin near the fingernail what invisible emanation may be coming from inside. Is it warm? Is it cold? Does it vibrate slightly, like electricity? In fact, why not, what the hell, what harm can it do just to touch it lightly, just once? Very quickly. After all, this is only the outer wrapping, neutral, like any other wrapper, hard (or soft?), smooth (or just a tiny bit rough, like the green baize on that billiard table?) and flat (or are there perhaps invisible protuberances that might give your finger some unimagined hints?). What harm can touching do? Just very lightly, hardly touching at all. As if you were feeling a bench or a fence that says 'wet paint'.

In fact, why not something more than a touch: a cautious prod? Gently. Like a doctor's hand carefully feeling the stomach to find out where it hurts, whether it is soft or tense. Or like a finger carefully feeling a pear: is it ripe? Hard? Almost ripe? In fact, what's wrong with taking it off the shelf for a moment? Just for ten seconds, or less, just to weigh it in your hand? To check if it's light or heavy? Is it dense? Or stiff? Is it like a lexicon? Or like a paperbound periodical? Or is it like a fragile glass object that is wrapped in straw or cotton-wool or sawdust, so that you can feel the softness of the wrapping material and the hardness of the object itself through the soft wrapping? Or is it full of dull heaviness pulling downwards, like a casket full of lead? Or will it turn out to be something furlike, responding and yielding to your fingers through the brown wrapping paper, pliant between your hands, like a cushion, a teddy bear, a cat? What on earth can it be? Just a hint of a touch, there, a kiss with the fingertip, just a touch like mist, like lips, and just a little stroke, hardly a stroke at all, so, yes, then a tiny prod, very quickly, and pull it out very slightly – like so – so that you can feel both sides of the package and finger the sticky paper, and what the hell, why not, take it right out of the bookcase and hold it in your arms for a moment, like a fighter carrying a comrade wounded in battle, only for heaven's sake be careful not to bump into the furniture, not to hit it, not to let it slip out of your grasp. And for god's sake don't forget which side was on top. And remember to use your handkerchief so as not to leave fingerprints, and then change the handkerchief in case it has absorbed some emanation.

It turned out that the package was cool and quite hard, oblong, exactly like a book wrapped in paper, smooth but not slippery. Its weight, too, seemed like that of a thick book: lighter than the concordance but a little heavier than the gazetteer.

And that, I hoped, was the end of that. I was freed. The temptations had had their prey and now they could go away, satisfied, and I could get on with my work at last.

I was mistaken.

It was the exact opposite.

Like a pack of hounds that have smelled bloody flesh, have had a taste of it and turned into wolves, ten minutes after I put the package back in its place, the temptations attacked me unexpectedly on an exposed flank:

To summon Ben Hur. Let him come here.

To let him into the secret of what we were hiding here. If he didn't believe me, then I'd show him the package and stun him so that at last, just for once, I'd see with my own eyes the outward indifference of the leopard turning to stunned amazement. Those tyrannical thin lips, normally too lazy to open, would gape wide with astonishment. At once, like morning mist that dissolves with the heat of the sun, the Orient Palace affair would melt away. I would force him to swear that he would never reveal what he had seen. Not even to Chita. And, in any case, he would only be allowed to take one look at the package, and then he must immediately forget what he had seen.

But he wouldn't forget. Ever. And so, in the shadow of the threat of imprisonment that would henceforth hang over the

85

two of us, we would be bound together once more by a strong, openhearted friendship. Like David and Jonathan. Together we would spy and collect secrets. We would even learn English together from Sergeant Dunlop, because a man who controls the enemy's language also controls his ways of thinking.

I suddenly had a strange, almost unbearable feeling that here, alone in this apartment all morning and all afternoon, I was the only ruler of a ferocious typhoon that was slumbering inside an outwardly innocent package, quite well camouflaged among the gems of literature on that shelf.

No. There was no question of bringing in Ben Hur. I would do it on my own. Without him.

Towards midday new, crazy temptations broke out like a thunderstorm in my chest and stomach: everything is in your power now. From now on, if you really want it, everything is possible. Everything depends on your wish. Take this unique package. You can put another package just like it, a book wrapped in identical paper, in its place on the shelf among the gems of literature, and no one will be the wiser. Not even Father.

As for you, son of man, pick up this destructive device, put it in your schoolbag and take it straight to Government House. Fix it with wire underneath the High Commissioner's car in the car park. Or stand waiting for him by the gate, and when he comes out throw it at his feet.

Or else: Hebrew youth from Jerusalem blows himself up to rouse the conscience of the world and to protest against the rape of his homeland.

Or maybe innocently ask Sergeant Dunlop to place the present in the CID commander's office? No: he might get blown up or implicated himself.

Or I could fit it to the tip of our rocket and threaten to blow London off the map if Jerusalem is not liberated.

Or eliminate Ben Hur and Chita. That'd show them.

And so on and so forth, until one o'clock, when a new and terrifying temptation raised its venomous head. And started to burrow and gnaw blindly inside me like a mole. (I found in the dictionary the proper word for this sucking, suckling temptation to cast off restraint and yield to the call of sin: it is 'seduction'. Like a cross between 'sedition' and 'suction'.)

This seductive urge clung to me relentlessly, pulling at my heart and my diaphragm through my ribs, penetrating my deepest recesses, insisting hideously, pleading and winking ingratiatingly, whispering febrile promises, sweetness of corrupt delights, secret joys that I had never tasted or only tasted in my dreams:

To leave the package where it was among the gems of world literature, after all. Not to lay a finger on it.

To go out. Lock the apartment. Go straight to the Orient Palace.

If he wasn't there, then drop it. It would be a sign. But if he was there, it would be a sign that I had to go ahead with it. It would be a sign that it had to be, that come what may this cloying sweetness had to overflow and take shape.

Tell him what was hidden in our apartment.

Ask him what to do about it.

And do whatever he told me.

Seduction.

Just before four o'clock there was a moment when I almost.

But I managed to resist. Instead of going to the Orient Palace, I ate a meatball and some beans from the icebox as well as a couple of potatoes, all cold: I didn't have the patience to heat it up. Then I closed my parents' door from the outside and my own bedroom door from the inside and lay down, not on my bed but on the cold floor in the cell-like space between my bed and my wardrobe and there, by the striped light that filtered like a ladder of shadows through the slats of the shutter, I read for an hour and a half. I knew the book already: it was about Magellan and Vasco da Gama, about islands and bays and volcanoes and thickly forested heights.

19

I SHALL NEVER FORGET the pangs of fear: like a ring of cold steel tightening round my fluttering heart. Very early, after the newspaper boy but before the milkman, in the middle of the dawn chorus, a British armoured car drove down the street with a loudspeaker and woke me up. Woke us all up. They announced in English and Hebrew a curfew from half past six until further notice. Anyone found outside would be risking his life.

Barefoot, with gummed eyes, I crawled into my parents' bed. I felt frozen, not with cold, but with the python's grip of foreboding: They'll find it. At once. What a ridiculous hiding place. It's not a hiding place at all, just a light-brown package stuck into a row of books with slightly less light-brown jackets. It stands out among the books because it is thicker and wider and taller, like a bandit who has wrapped himself in sackcloth and thrust himself into a procession of nuns. Father and Mother would be locked up in the Russian Compound, or taken to Acre gaol. They might even be deported in handcuffs to Cyprus or Mauritius or Eritrea, or possibly to the Seychelles. The word 'banishment' pierced my chest like a stiletto.

And what would I do all alone in this apartment, knowing as well as I did how quickly it could change from being small and pleasant to being huge and sinister, in the nights, weeks, and years to come, alone at home, alone in Jerusalem, and alone altogether since my grandparents (both sets), aunts and uncles were all murdered by Hitler, and they would murder me too when they got here and dragged me out of my wretched hiding place in the broom-cupboard. Anti-semitic drunken British soldiers, or bloodthirsty Arab gangs. Because we are the few and we are in the right and we always were in the right but we were always few, surrounded on all sides and without a friend in the world. (Apart from Sergeant Dunlop? And you go spying on him and stealing secrets from him. Traitor traitor. You're doomed.)

For a few moments we lay there in bed, the three of us. We did not speak. Then Father's quiet voice came, a voice that seemed to paint in the darkness of the room a ring of common sense:

'The paper. We still have another thirty-two minutes. I definitely have time to go and fetch the paper.'

My mother said:

'Please stay. Don't go.'

I backed her up, trying to make my voice more like his than like hers:

'Yes, really, Dad, don't go. It's definitely not rational to take risks for a newspaper.'

He came back a moment later, still in his blue pyjamas and his black open-backed sandals, smiling self-deprecatingly, as if he had returned from hunting a lion in the jungle for us. And he handed the paper to my mother.

I helped them to fold away their bed, which as soon as it was closed pretended to be an honest sofa. Nothing suspicious about me, don't even imagine that I have a totally private inner side, hidden mattresses, pillows, sheets, and a nightie. Never heard of them.

I scattered the five cushions on the sofa, spacing them out precisely. I made my own bed too. We managed to wash and dress and tidy everything away and straighten the tablecloth and even to hide my mother's slippers under the sofa, all the time, by some unspoken agreement, taking care to avoid looking in the direction of the package, which for some reason had decided in the night to make itself conspicuous. It stood out among the gems of world literature in Polish like a clumsy soldier at morning roll call in high-school. Just at the moment when my mother was about to straighten the flowers in the

89

vase and Father was changing the paper in the blotter on his desk and I had been sent to the kitchen to set the table, the knock on the door came. An English voice asked if there was anyone in, please. Father replied at once, also in English, and also politely:

'Just a minute, please.'

And he opened the door.

I was surprised to see that there were only three of them: two ordinary soldiers (one of them had a burn mark that made half his face red, like butcher's meat), and a young officer with a narrow chest and a long narrow face. All three were wearing long shorts and khaki socks that almost met the shorts in the region of the knee. The two soldiers were armed with tommy guns whose barrels were pointing at the ground, as though lowering their eyes, and rightly, in shame. The officer was holding a pistol, also pointing downwards; it looked just like Sergeant Dunlop's. (Maybe they were acquaintances or friends of his? What if I told them right away that I was a friend of the Sergeant's? Would they abandon the search, and even join us for breakfast? So that we could talk to them, and finally open their eyes to the injustice they were inflicting on us.)

Father pronounced the words 'Please come in' with particular and emphatic courtesy. The thin officer was startled for an instant, as if Father's courtesy converted the search of this apartment into an act of extreme rudeness. He begged our pardon for disturbing us so early in the morning, explained that unfortunately it was his duty to have a quick look round and make sure everything was as it should be, and without thinking he put his pistol back into its holster and buttoned it up.

There was a moment's hesitation, on their side and on ours: it was not clear how we should proceed. Was there anything else that needed to be said, on our side or on theirs, before the inspection could go on?

Whenever young Dr Gryphius at the clinic in Obadiah Street examined me she always had difficulty finding the right words to ask me to strip down to my underpants. My mother and I would stand waiting patiently while she summoned up

90

the courage to say in gravelly German Hebrew: 'Take off please all the clothes only there is no need to take off the underwear.' As she spoke the word 'underwear' it was plain that she was extremely uneasy. As if she felt that there ought to be another, less ugly, less incisive word (and in fact I believe she was right). A short while after the setting up of the State, Dr Gryphius fell in love with a blind Armenian poet and followed him to Cyprus; three years later she returned alone and reappeared in our clinic. She had acquired a new look: there was something bitter and thin about her. Although in fact she had not got thinner; she had shrunk, shrivelled. But as I said earlier, I cannot live or even get to sleep without order. Hence Magda Gryphius and her blind Armenian poet and the flute she brought back from Famagusta and the strange tunes she sometimes played at two or three in the morning, and also her second husband, who was an importer of confectionery and inventor of a potion against forgetfulness, and also the whole question of suitable and unsuitable words for private parts of the body and intimate items of clothing will all have to wait for another story.

The officer turned respectfully toward Father, like a polite schoolboy addressing a teacher:

'Excuse me. We'll make a special effort to be brief, but in the meantime I'm afraid I must ask you all not to leave this spot.'

My mother said:

'Can I make you a cup of tea?'

The officer replied apologetically:

'No, thank you. I'm on duty.'

And Father, in Hebrew, in his steady, correct voice, protested:

'You're overdoing it. That was unnecessary.'

The search itself did not win my approbation, from a professional point of view. (I had surreptitiously inched forward another four or five feet, to the corner of the hallway, which gave me a vantage point commanding most of the apartment.)

The soldiers peered under my bed, opened the wardrobe in my bedroom, pushed the clothes' hangers aside, prodded around in the shelves of shirts and underwear, glanced into the kitchen and very cursorily into the bathroom, concentrated for some reason on the icebox, examined the area above, underneath, and behind it, tapped the walls in two places, and in the meantime the officer inspected Father's wall maps. The soldier with the burned face discovered a loose coat hook in the hallway, and tested to see how loose it was, until the officer growled that if he wasn't careful he'd break it. The soldier obediently left it alone. When they all entered my parents' bedroom, we followed them. Apparently the officer had forgotten that we were supposed to stay in a corner of the hallway. The extent of the library clearly startled him, and he hesitantly asked Father: 'Excuse me, is this a school? Or is it a place of worship?'

Father hurriedly offered an explanation, and a guided tour. My mother whispered to him, 'Don't get carried away,' but in vain. He was already swept on a mounting tide of pedagogy and started to explain in English:

'This is a strictly private library. For purposes of research, sir.'

The officer did not seem to understand. He inquired politely whether Father was a bookseller. Or a bookbinder.

'No, a scholar, sir.' Father spoke emphatically, syllable by syllable, in that Slavic English of his. And he added: 'An historian.'

'Interesting,' remarked the officer, his face reddening as though he had been reprimanded.

After a moment, as his self-respect returned and he perhaps recalled his rank and his task, he repeated firmly:

'Very interesting.'

Then he asked if there were any books in English. His question offended Father, but also excited him. It was like throwing live ammunition on a bonfire. With one shot the arrogant officer had wounded both Father's pride as book collector and scholar and our historic standing as one of the great cultured peoples of the world. Did that conceited *goy* imagine he was in some native hovel in a Malayan village? Or in a hut full of Ugandan tribesmen?

At once, brimming and overflowing with enthusiasm, as though he were defending the very claims of Zionism, Father started to pull down one English book after another, announcing aloud the title and date of publication and the edition, and thrusting them one by one into the officer's arms, as though he were formally introducing long-established guests to a new arrival at the party. 'Lord Byron, Edinburgh edition. Milton. Shelley and Keats. And here is an edition of Chaucer with a commentary. Robert Browning, an early limited edition. Complete Shakespeare: Johnson, Steevens and Reed edition. And here, on this shelf, is where the philosophers live: here is Bacon, Mill, Adam Smith, John Locke, Bishop Berkeley, and the incomparable David Hume. And here is a luxury edition of –'

The officer, reassured, unbent somewhat, and from time to time he found the courage to extend a cautious finger and gently touch the coats of these fellow countrymen. Meanwhile, Father triumphantly darted backwards and forwards between the visitor and the bookshelves, pulling out books left right and centre and handing him more and more of them. Mother repeatedly tried to signal to him with desperate grimaces from where she stood next to the sofa that in another moment he would bring disaster on us all with his own hands.

In vain.

Father forgot everything: he forgot the package, he forgot the Underground, he forgot the sufferings of our people, and he forgot those who rise up against us in every generation to annihilate us; he forgot my mother and me. He was transported to unimaginable heights of missionary ecstasy: if he could only manage finally to convince the British, who were a fundamentally civilized and moral people, that we, their subjects suffering here in a far-flung corner of the Empire, are really wonderful, cultured, civilized, book-reading, poetry- and philosophy-loving people, then at once they would undergo a change of heart and all the misunderstandings would be removed. Then at last both they and we would be free to sit face to face and talk to one another properly about things that were, when all was said and done, the meaning and purpose of life.

Once or twice the officer tried to get a word in edgeways,

to ask a question, or perhaps only to take his leave and get on with doing his duty, but no force in the world could halt Father in full spate: blind and deaf to the world, he continued with the ardour of a zealot revealing the treasures of his shrine.

The thin officer could only murmur from time to time, 'Indeed' or 'How very interesting', as though he was under a spell. The two soldiers in the passage began to whisper to each other. The burned one stared foolishly at my mother. His friend chuckled and scratched himself. Mother, for her part, had seized the hem of the curtain and her fingers were moving desperately from one pleat to the next, straightening, kneading, stretching each pleat separately.

How about me?

My duty was to find some secret way of warning Father, who was gradually drawing the British officer towards the deadly shelf. But how could I? All I was able to do was at least not to look in the direction it was better not to look. Suddenly the brown paper package succumbed to an urge to turn traitor: it started to make itself conspicuous, to stand out in the row of books, like a fang among milk teeth, looking out of place and different from the others in colour, height, and thickness.

Seduction suddenly took hold of me again. As happens to me sometimes in Mr Zerubbabel Gihon's thunderous Bible lessons, when it starts with a little sensation in my chest, a tickle in my throat, nothing to speak of, it stirs and stops and stirs again and starts to get stronger and press against the sluice gates; in vain I try to last another minute, another second, press my lips together, clench my teeth, tense my muscles, but the laughter bursts out like a cascade, gushes out, so that I have to rush out of the classroom. The same thing happened that morning of the search, only it was not a tickle of laughter, but a tickle of betrayal. Seduction.

Just as when you feel a sneeze coming, and it starts by trickling out of your brain and pinching the base of your nose till it brings tears to your eyes, and even if you try to smother it, it's obvious that you haven't a hope, that it's bound to happen, so I started to guide the enemy towards the package that the Underground had asked us to hide, the package that apparently contained the detonation device of the Hebrew atom bomb, which had the potential to liberate us now and for all time from the destiny of being forever defenceless lambs at the mercy of wolves.

'Quite warm,' I said.

Then:

'Very warm.' 'Cooler.' 'Lukewarm.' 'Colder again.' 'Freezing.'

And a little later:

'Getting warmer. Warmer. Hot. Nearly burning.'

I can't explain it. Even today. It may have been a vague wish that the thing that was bound to happen should finally happen. And would stop hanging like a rock above our heads. Like having a wisdom tooth extracted: let's get it over with.

Because it's unbearable.

Nevertheless, my sense of responsibility got the better of me. I didn't say my hot and cold out loud, but only inside, behind my sealed lips.

The English officer gently deposited on the coffee table the mountain of books that had been piled up in his arms and almost reached his chin. He thanked Father twice, apologized again to my mother for the unpleasantness and the nuisance, and rebuked in a whisper one of the soldiers who was touching a wall map with his finger. As they were leaving, when they were through the door but it had not yet closed behind them, he turned to look at me, and suddenly he gave me a wink, as if to say:

Well, what can we do?

And off they went.

Two days later the general curfew was cancelled and once again there was only a night curfew. The rumour went round the neighbourhood that in Mr Vitkin's flat, Mr Vitkin from Barclay's Bank, they had found a pistol magazine full of bullets. They said he was taken off in handcuffs to the Russian Compound. And the brown paper package disappeared from among the gems of world literature after a couple of days. It had evaporated. There was no gap in the shelf. As if it had all been a dream.

20

WITHDRAWN FROM STOCK

I HAVE ALREADY EXPLAINED about the locked medicine drawer and my mother's role in the Underground. During the night curfew, when I was woken by shooting or the rumble of an explosion, I would sometimes try not to fall asleep again even when silence returned. Tensely I lay there hoping to catch the sound of hurried footfalls on the pavement outside my window, a scratching at the door, whispered voices in the hallway, groans of pain stifled by clenched teeth. It was my duty not to know who had been injured. Not to see, not to hear a thing, not even to try to imagine the spare mattress being spread out on the kitchen floor in the night, only to disappear before day dawned.

All that summer I waited. No wounded fighter ever came.

Four days before the end of the summer holidays, before I started in the seventh year, my parents went to Tel Aviv to take part in a memorial evening for the town they had come from.

My mother said:

'Listen carefully. Yardena has offered to spend the night here to look after you because we are sleeping over in Tel Aviv. Be as good as gold. Don't be a nuisance. Help Yardena. Eat what's put on your plate, don't forget there are dead children in the world who would have lived for another week if they had only had the food you leave on your plate.'

There's a pit inside the stomach that science hasn't discovered yet, and all the blood drained into that pit from my head, my heart, my knees, and turned into an ocean and roared like the ocean.

I summoned up what was left of my voice and answered, folding the newspaper that was lying on the table into two, four, eight:

'It'll be fine. You go.'

And I tried to fold it in half again but I couldn't.

The question I was asking myself as I folded the paper was whether science had discovered, and if not whether I myself could discover within the next couple of hours, a way of making someone disappear without trace for twenty-four hours or so. Vanish completely. Not exist. Not just to be vacant, like, say, the spaces between the stars, but to vanish and yet to go on being here, to see and hear everything. To be me and also a shadow. Be present without being present.

Because what was I going to do alone with Yardena? What could I do about my shame? And in our home, too? Should I ask her to forgive me? Before or after finding out (how can you find out, fool?) whether or not she looked out and noticed somebody watching her from the roof on the opposite side of the street? And if she did, whether she noticed who it was? Did I really have to confess? And if so, how could I convince her that it was just an accident? That I really didn't see anything. That I definitely wasn't the notorious peeping tom who had been seen on the roofs in our neighbourhood and that people talked about in whispers and had been trying to catch without success for several months now. And that when I saw her (only once! only for about ten seconds!) I wasn't thinking about her body but the schemes of the British occupier? That it was just an accident? (What was? What did I see? Nothing. A dark patch, a bright patch, another dark patch.) Perhaps I should tell her a lie? What lie? How? And what about the thoughts I'd had about her since then?

I'd do better to keep my mouth shut.

We'd both do better to try to pretend that what happened didn't happen. Just as my parents said nothing about the package that was hidden here during the search. Just as they said nothing about lots of things, those silences that were like bites.

My parents set off at three, not before extracting a whole string of promises from me: Remember, be careful, don't forget, make sure, on no account, take special care, heaven forbid. As they left they said:

'The icebox is full of food and don't forget to show her where everything is and be nice and helpful and don't be a nuisance. And remember specially to tell her that the sofa in our room is made up as a bed for her and tell her there's a note for her in the kitchen and that the icebox is full, and you're to be in bed by ten and remember to lock the front door with both keys and remind her to turn the lights out.'

I was alone. I waited. A hundred times I went round each room making sure it was all tidy and nothing was out of place. I was afraid and yet somehow hoping that she might have forgotten she had promised to come. Or that she wouldn't make it before the curfew started and I'd be on my own all night. Then I got my mother's sewing basket out of the wardrobe and sewed a button on my shirt, not because it had come off but because it was loose and I didn't want it to fall off just when Yardena was here. Then I cleared away the spent matches that we kept in a separate box next to the new ones to reuse, as an economy measure, for lighting the paraffin cooker from the primus or vice versa. I hid them right at the back, behind the spices, because I was afraid that Yardena would see them and think we were poor or mean or not very tidy. Then I stood in front of the full-length mirror on the back of the wardrobe door, breathing the faint scent of mothballs that always clung to the wardrobe and made me think of winter. I looked at the mirror for a while and tried to decide once and for all, objectively, as Father demanded, what I looked like.

I looked like a pale, thin, angular child, with a face that was always changing and with very restless eyes.

Is that the look of a traitor?

Or of a panther in the basement?

I felt a sad pain at the thought that Yardena was already almost grown up.

If only she could really know me, she might realize that I am simply trapped inside the shell of a talkative child, but that inside, peeping out –

No: better stop there. The word peeping hurt like a slap round the face. Which I well deserved. If it somehow came out that Yardena felt like giving me my slap this evening, I might actually feel better. I hope she's forgotten, I hope she'll never come, I thought, and I ran to peep – no not peep – take a look, from the corner of the bathroom window, because from there you could almost see as far as the Sinopsky Brothers grocery shop on the corner. Since I was in the bathroom, I decided to wash my face and neck, not with the ordinary soap that Father and I used, but with my mother's scented soap. Next I wet my hair with water and combed it and straightened my parting, then I fanned my head with the paper, to dry my hair quickly, because what would happen if Yardena arrived at this very moment and realized I had wet my hair just for her. I cut my fingernails a bit, too, even though I'd already cut them on Friday, just to be on the safe side, but I was sorry I'd done it because now my fingernails looked as if I'd been chewing them.

I waited till nine minutes to seven. The curfew was about to begin. Several times since then I've found myself waiting for a woman and wondering whether or not she would come, and if she did, what we would do, and what I looked like, and what I should say to her, but no wait was ever as tense and cruel as that time, when Yardena almost didn't turn up.

I have just written the words 'waiting for a woman', because Yardena was then almost twenty whereas I was twelve and a quarter, which was barely sixty-two percent of her age; in other words, we were separated by thirty-eight percent of her age, as I calculated with a pencil on one of the blank cards from Father's desk as the clock approached seven and the beginning of the curfew, and I had convinced myself that that was that, there was no hope, Yardena had forgotten me, and with good reason.

I worked it out like this: In another ten years, when I reached the age of twenty-two and a quarter, and Yardena was thirty, I would still be only seventy-four percent of her age, which was definitely better than the current sixty-two percent but still pretty grim. As the years went on the distance between us would gradually decrease (in percentages), but the depressing part was that this decreasing gap would decrease more and more slowly. Like an exhausted marathon runner. I went over the calculation three times, and each time the gap decreased more and more slowly. It seemed to me completely unfair and illogical that in the years immediately ahead I would go leaping towards her in tens of percents and then, in our years of middle age and old age, the percentage gap between us would decrease at a snail's pace. Why? And was it impossible for the decreasing gap to be closed completely? Ever? (Laws of nature. OK. I know. But when my mother told me her story about the blue shutter, she said that in the old days the laws of nature were completely different. There was a time when the earth was flat and the sun and the stars revolved around it. Now all we had left revolving round us was our own moon, and who knew if that law, too, wouldn't be revoked some day in the future? It followed that change in general was always change for the worse.)

When Yardena was a hundred, I worked out, I would be ninety-two and a quarter, and the percentage gap between us would be reduced to less than eight (which was not bad, compared to the thirty-eight of this evening). But what good would the decreasing gap between our ages be to a decrepit old couple?

I switched off this thought and the desk lamp, tore up the calculations and threw them in the toilet, then pulled the chain, and since I was in the bathroom anyway I decided to brush my teeth. While I was brushing them I made up my mind to be different: from now on I would be a quiet, straightforward, logical and above all brave man. In other words: if a last-minute miracle happened and Yardena really did turn up after all, even though the curfew had almost begun, I would say to her straight out, simply and succinctly, that I was sorry about what happened on the roof and it wouldn't happen again. Ever.

But how could I?

She arrived at five to seven. She had brought us fresh-baked rolls from Angel's Bakery, where she worked as a clerk. She was wearing a light sleeveless summer frock, with a pattern of cyclamens and a row of big buttons all the way down the front, like polished river pebbles arranged in a row by a child. She said:

'Ben Hur didn't want to come. He wouldn't say what's happened. What's up between you, Proffy? Have you had another row?'

All the blood that had drained into the pit under my stomach gushed up and flushed hotly into my face and ears. Even my own blood was betraying me, and embarrassing me in front of Yardena. What is closer to a man than his own blood? And now even my blood had turned traitor.

'It wasn't a personal row; it was a rift.'

Yardena said:

'Ah. A rift. Proffy whenever you use words like that you sound just like Voice of Fighting Zion. And where are your own words? Haven't you got any words of your own? Didn't you ever have any?'

'Look,' I said very seriously.

And a few moments later I repeated:

'Look.'

'There's nothing much to look at.'

'What I wanted you to know, and this doesn't concern your brother, but questions of principle –'

'OK, fine. Questions of principle. If you like we'll have a discussion later about the extent of the rift in the Underground and the questions of principle. But not now, Proffy.' (Underground?! How much did she know about us? And who had dared to tell her? Or was she just guessing?) 'Later. Right now I'm famished. Let's fix ourselves a wild supper. Not just a salad and yoghurt. Something much more exciting.' She scrutinized the kitchen thoroughly, peering into cupboards and drawers, casting an eye over the pots and pans, investigating the icebox, checking the spices and condiments, examining the two paraffin burners. Then she pondered for a while, making all sorts of vague sounds to herself, *mmm* and *ouf* and *ahh*, and then, still sunk in thought like a general devising battle plans, she instructed me to start preparing some vegetables – no, not there, over here – tomatoes, green peppers, onions, about this much. Then she put the chopping board down on the counter, took the big butcher's knife out of the drawer, and discovering the pot of chicken soup that my mother had left for us in the icebox she took a cupful of it. Then she cut the chicken in pieces, and heated some oil in a frying pan. She laid the vegetables I had prepared for her on a corner of the draining board. When the oil began to bubble,

101

she fried some cloves of garlic in it and browned the chicken pieces on both sides, until the mingled smells of chicken, garlic, and hot oil made my mouth water and sent urgent spasms through my palate, throat, and stomach. Yardena said:

'Why haven't you got any olives? I don't mean those olives from a jar, silly, those vegetarian olives. Why haven't you got any decadent olives, the sort that make you a bit tipsy? When you find some real olives, bring me some. You can even wake me up in the middle of the night.' (I did find some. Years later. But I was too shy to take her olives in the middle of the night.)

When she decided the chicken pieces were brown enough, she took them out of the frying pan and laid them on a serving dish, then she washed and dried the frying pan.

'Wait a minute, Proffy,' she said. 'Hang on. This is only the curtain-raiser. Meanwhile, why don't you set the table?'

Then she heated some more oil in the pan and, leaving the fragrant garlic-scented chicken pieces to wait, she fried the finely-chopped onion, and while the onion turned golden and then brown in front of my staring eyes, she added the little pieces of tomato and pepper that were waiting for her on the draining board, sprinkled some chopped parsley over it all, and mixed the ingredients together well as she fried them. Soon my soul was in an agony of anticipation at the delightful smells, and I thought I couldn't endure another minute, another second, another breath, but Yardena laughed and told me not to touch the rolls or anything, it would be a pity to spoil my appetite, what's the matter with you, what's your hurry, contain yourself. And she put the chicken pieces back in the frying pan and rolled them around in the oil until it soaked right through to the bone, and only then did she pour the cupful of soup over them. She waited for it to boil.

Seventy-seven years of agony went past, as slow as torture, to the limit of endurance and beyond, and further to the point of despair, and further still till the heart sobbed, before the stock began to bubble and boil, and the oil began to splutter and spit. Yardena turned the heat down and sprinkled on some salt and a pinch of ground black pepper. Then she put the lid on the pan, leaving a small space for the tantalizing vapours to escape. While the broth was boiling she added

102

some little cubes of potato and some even smaller cubes of hot red pepper. She waited ruthlessly until the broth evaporated, leaving behind a heavenly thick sauce enfolding the pieces of fried chicken that seemed to have grown wings and become a psalm and a dream. The whole apartment was astonished at the bevy of powerful smells wafting from the kitchen and invading every corner like frantic rioters. Such odours had not been smelled here since the building was built.

Meanwhile, aflame with desire and anticipation and pangs of hunger, swallowing back the surging saliva, I laid the table for the two of us, facing each other like Mother and Father. I decided to leave my usual place empty. As I laid the table I could see Yardena out of the corner of my eye tossing the chicken pieces in the frying pan, to remind them who they were, tasting the sauce, adjusting the seasoning, spooning it over the food which had taken on a wonderful hue of burnished brass or old gold, and her arms, her shoulders, and her hips came alive in a kind of dance inside her dress, protected by my mother's apron, as though the chicken pieces were shaking her while she shook them.

When we had eaten our fill, we sat facing each other picking at a bunch of sweet grapes; then we devoured half a watermelon and drank coffee together even though I told Yardena honestly and bravely that I wasn't allowed coffee, especially in the evening before going to bed.

Yardena said:

'They're not here.'

And she also said:

'Now for a cigarette. Just me. Not you. Find me an ashtray.' But there was no ashtray, and there couldn't be one, because smoking was forbidden in our apartment. Always. Under any circumstances. Even visitors were forbidden to smoke. Father was fundamentally opposed to the very idea of smoking. He also held firmly to the view that visitors should observe the rules of the house, like a traveller in a foreign land. He supported this view with a proverb that he was fond of citing, about how to behave when in Rome. (Years later, when I visited Rome for the first time, I was astonished to discover that it was full of smokers. But when Father said Rome, he generally

103

meant ancient Rome, not the Rome that exists today.)

Yardena smoked two cigarettes and drank two cups of coffee (I was only given one). While she smoked she stuck her legs out in front of her and rested her feet on my chair, which was empty this evening. I decided it was my duty to get up at once, clear the table, put the leftover food away in the icebox, and wash up. The only thing I couldn't do was to take the rubbish outside, because of the curfew.

Who has ever spent a whole night alone in an apartment with a girl, while outside there is a night curfew and all the streets are deserted and the whole city is bolted and barred? When you know that nobody in the world can disturb you? And a deep, wide silence hangs over the night like a mist?

I stood over the kitchen sink, scouring the bottom of the frying pan with steel wool, with my back to Yardena and my soul the exact opposite (its back to the sink and the frying pan and all its being facing towards Yardena). Suddenly I said quickly, with my eyes tight closed, as if I were swallowing a pill:

'Anyway I'm sorry about what happened that time. On the roof. It won't ever happen again.'

Yardena said to my back:

'Of course it will. And how! Only at least try to make it a bit less stupid than the way it was that time.'

A single fly was sitting on the edge of a cup. I wished I could change places with it.

Then, still in the kitchen (Yardena used her saucer as an ashtray), she asked me to explain to her, in a nutshell, what my row with her brother was all about. Sorry, not row, rift.

My duty was to say nothing. To maintain the cloak of secrecy, even under torture. I had seen in lots of films how women extract secrets even from very strong men, like Gary Cooper or even Douglas Fairbanks. And in Bible class Mr Gihon said, at his wife's expense: 'Samson was destroyed because he fell into the clutches of a wicked woman.' You might have thought that after all the times I had seethed with rage watching films where the men succumbed and started spilling the beans to women, and something terrible always happened, the same thing definitely would not happen to me. But that night I couldn't stop myself either: it was as though another Proffy had sprouted inside me and started gushing forth light-headedly, as it says in the Bible, as though suddenly all the fountains of the great deep were opened. This other Proffy started telling her everything and I could not stop him, even though I tried as hard as I could and I pleaded with him to stop, but he only shrugged, and made fun of me: Yardena already knows anyway, she explicitly said 'your Underground', Ben Hur is the traitor, and you and I are both in the clear.

This inner Proffy hid nothing from Yardena. The Underground. The split. The rocket. Mother's locked drawer and Father's Perfidious Albion slogans. The package. The temptation. The seduction. Not even Sergeant Dunlop. Was I high on some essence or drug that Yardena had slipped into the fried chicken pieces? Or her witches' brew of a sauce? Or drunk on her coffee, which was strong and harsh? That was how the lame detective was drugged in the film *Panther in the Basement*. (But he was a secondary character. Naturally they failed to drug the hero himself.)

What if she was a double agent? Or suppose she had been sent by Ben Hur's special unit for Internal Security and Interrogation? (To which the inner Proffy answered mockingly: 'So what? What secrets are there left to keep between a traitor and a traitress?')

Yardena said:

'That's cute.'

And then she said:

'What's really special about you is that whenever you describe something I can see it in front of my eyes.'

And she touched me on my left shoulder, quite close to the base of my arm, and added:

'Don't be sad. Just wait quietly and don't suck up to him. Ben Hur will have to come back to you because without you, just think, who has he got left to dominate? And he simply has to dominate someone. He can't get to sleep at night without dominating somebody first. That's the trouble with dominating: once you've started you can't really stop. Don't you worry, Proffy, because I don't think you'll catch it. Even though it is quite contagious. And besides –'

She stopped. She lit another cigarette and smiled, not to me but perhaps to herself, a sort of smile of inner amusement, a smile that doesn't know it exists.

'And besides what?' I dared to ask.

'Nothing. Undergrounds and all that sort of thing. Remind me what we were talking about. Weren't we talking about undergrounds?'

The right answer was: No. Because before she stopped to light her cigarette we had been talking about the urge to dominate. Despite which I said:

'Yes. Undergrounds.'

Yardena said:

'Undergrounds. Forget about undergrounds. You'd be better advised to go on peeping, only more cleverly than that time. And better still, Proffy, instead of peeping, you should learn to ask. If you know how to ask, you don't need to peep. The trouble is that, apart from in the movies, there's almost no man who knows how to ask. That's how it is in this country, anyway. Instead of asking, either they get down on all fours and beg, or they put pressure on you, or they cheat. And that's without even mentioning vulgar gropers, who are almost the majority here. Maybe you will. One day. That is, maybe one day you will learn how to ask. In fact, even if people do sometimes go mad and die from this boy and girl and love business, it's much more likely to happen from undergrounds and all that salvation nonsense. Don't believe what you see in the movies. In real life people ask for all sorts of things, but they don't ask for them the right way. Then they stop asking and only give and take offence. In the end they get used to it all and stop bothering, and when that happens there's no more time. Life is over.'

'Do you want a cushion?' I asked. 'My mother likes to sit in the kitchen in the evening with a cushion behind her back.'

Yardena's nearly twenty, and she still has that little-girl habit of adjusting the hem of her dress as though her knee is a baby that she has to cover up over and over again, just right, not too little or it'll catch cold, and not too much or it won't have enough air to breathe.

'My brother,' she said, 'your friend, will never have a friend. Specially not a girlfriend. Only subjects. And women.

106

He'll have plenty of women, because the world is awash with poor wretches who throw themselves under tyrants' feet. But he won't have a woman friend. Get me a glass of water would you, Proffy. Not from the tap, from the icebox. Actually, I'm not thirsty. You will have women friends. And I'll tell you why. It's because whenever you're given something, even if it's nothing more than a roll, or a paper napkin, or a teaspoon, you behave as if you've been given a present. As if a miracle has occurred.'

I didn't agree with her about everything but I decided not to argue. Except about one point, earlier in the conversation, a point I could on no account pass over in silence:

'But, Yardena, what you were saying before about undergrounds, surely without the Underground the English will never let us have the Land.'

She suddenly burst out laughing, a wide-open, musical laughter that only girls who enjoy being girls have. And she tried to sweep her cigarette smoke away with her hand, as though it were a fly:

'There you go again,' she said, 'talking like the Voice of Fighting Zion. You aren't an underground, you and Ben Hur and what's-his-name, the other one, the little monkey. An underground is something completely different. Something awesome. Something lethal. Even when there really isn't any alternative and you have to fight, an underground is still something deadly. Besides which, these British may well pack up and go home soon. I only hope we don't regret it, regret it bitterly, when we're left here without them.'

These words seemed to me dangerously irresponsible. In some way they resembled Sergeant Dunlop's remark that the Arabs were the weaker side and soon they'd become the new Jews. What was the connection between what Yardena was saying and his opinion about the Arabs? None at all. And yet there was a connection. I was furious with myself for not being able to see what the connection was and with Yardena for saying things that were better left unsaid. Maybe it was my duty to tell some responsible adult about these thoughts? Father, perhaps? To warn them, so that those who needed to know would be aware that Yardena was a bit frivolous.

Even if I did decide to report what she had said, I mustn't arouse her suspicions.

I said:

'I have a different opinion. We must drive the British out of the Land by force.'

'We will,' said Yardena, 'but not tonight. Just look at the time, it's nearly a quarter to eleven, and, tell me, are you a sound sleeper?'

This question struck me as strange, and even a little suspicious. I replied cautiously:

'Yes. No. It depends.'

'Well tonight you'd better sleep soundly. And if you do happen to wake up, you can turn your light on and read till the morning for all I care. But don't you dare leave your room, because on the stroke of midnight if there's a moon I turn into a wolf, or more precisely a vampire, and I've already gobbled up a hundred kids like you. So, whatever you do, don't you open your door in the night. Promise.'

I promised. On my word of honour. But my suspicions deepened. I decided I must try not to fall asleep. And I thought it definitely wouldn't be difficult, because of the coffee I had drunk and the smell of smoke everywhere in the apartment and what Yardena had said about my strong side and other strange things.

In the hallway, after I had washed and before saying good night, she reached out suddenly and touched me on the head. Her hand was neither soft nor hard, quite different from my mother's. She ruffled my hair for a moment and said: 'Listen very carefully, Proffy. That sergeant you told me about. He sounds really nice, he may even happen to be fond of children, but I don't think you're in any danger, because he's an inhibited man. At least that's the way he comes across from your description. And by the way, since you're called Proffy, which is short for Professor, why don't you start being a professor instead of a spy or a general? Half the world are spies and generals. Not you. You're a word-child. Good night. And I'll tell you what I found really nice: that you washed all the dishes without me asking. Ben Hur only does the washing-up if he's bribed.'

21

BUT WHY DID I lock my bedroom door on the inside that night? Even now, more than forty years later, I do not know. I know even less now than I did at the time. (There are all manners and degrees of not knowing. Just as a window can be not just open or shut, but half open, or one part can be open and the rest shut, or it can be open just a crack, or be covered with a shutter on the outside and a thick curtain on the inside, or even fastened shut with nails.)

I locked my door and undressed with a firm resolve not to think the faintest thought about Yardena on the other side of the wall, who might be getting undressed at this very moment just like me, undoing one smooth round button after another down the front of her light sleeveless dress, and I made up my mind simply not to think about those buttons, not the top ones near her throat nor the bottom ones near her knees.

I switched on my bedside lamp and started looking at a book, but it was a little hard for me to concentrate. ('Instead of peeping, you should learn to ask.' What had she meant by that? And 'You're a word-child'! But how come? Hadn't she noticed that I was a panther in a basement?)

I put the book down and put out the light because it was almost midnight, but, instead of sleep, thoughts came, and to drive them away I switched on the light again and picked up the book. It didn't help.

That night was deep and wide. Not a cricket's chirp disturbed the curfew. Not a shot was heard. Little by little the submarines in the book turned into submarines made of fog, sailing slowly among banks of drifting fog. The sea was soft and warm. Then I was a mountain child building himself a hut from lumps of fog in the mountains, and suddenly there was a sort of nibbling or sawing at the edge of the hut, as though a stranded whale was scratching himself on the sandy sea bottom. I tried to silence it and I woke up to a sound of *shshsh*, and opening my eyes I found that I had fallen asleep with my light on, and that the shushing sound from the dream had not stopped. It was still going on.

In a flash I sat up in bed, as alert and wary as a robber. There were no death throes, no whale; this was the scratching in the night that I had been waiting for all that summer. A very light but urgent, persistent scratching. It was definitely coming from the entrance, from our front door. It was an injured Underground fighter, who might be dripping blood. We must dress his wound and lay him down in the kitchen on the spare mattress and he must be on his way just before day dawns. What about Father? Mother? Are they asleep? Can't they hear the urgent scratching at the door? Should I wake them? Or open the door myself? They're not here. They're away. There's Yardena, and I promised her on my word of honour not to leave my room. And I remembered how once, when I was nearly ten, she cleaned and dressed a wound I had and I was sorry the other knee wasn't cut too.

Then came the sound of footsteps, running barefoot along the passage. The thud of the bolt and the turning of the key in the lock. Whispers. And more footsteps. Rapid low conversation, from the direction of the kitchen now. The scrape of a match on a matchbox. A short rush of water from the tap. And other sounds that it was not easy to identify from where I was, in my bed. Then there was total velvety silence again. Had it all been just a dream? Or was it my duty to get up, break my promise, and go and find out what was going on?

Silence.

Phantom footsteps.

Suddenly the toilet cistern roared. Then the murmur of water rushing along the pipes in the wall. Then more dim voices and bare feet passing the door of my room, that was definitely Yardena whispering to her injured fighter, 'Wait a minute, shut up, wait there.' Then a grating sound from my parents' bedroom: furniture being moved? A drawer? And suddenly there was a sound of stifled laughter, and perhaps of sobbing, as though underwater.

When I am a wounded Underground fighter fleeing hot pursuit, will I also have the strength of character to laugh, like this man, when my wound is being cleaned and treated with a burning, stinging liquid and wrapped tightly with a bandage?

I suspected I wouldn't. And in the meantime the laughter on the other side of the wall turned into a groan and a few moments later Yardena groaned too. Then more sounds and whispers. And then silence. After a lot more darkness stray shots started up in the distance, spaced out as though they, too, were tired. And I may have fallen asleep.

22

THE ESSENCE OF treachery does not lie in the traitor suddenly getting up and leaving the close circle of the faithful. Only a superficial traitor does that. The real, deep-down traitor is the one who is right inside. In the heart of hearts: the one who most resembles and belongs, who is most involved. The one who is most like the others, even more so than the others. The one who really loves those he is betraying, because what betrayal is there without love? (I admit this is a complicated matter that belongs in another story. A truly organized man would cross out these lines or transfer them to a suitable story. Nevertheless, I am not going to cross them out. You can skip, if you like.)

That summer came to an end. At the beginning of September we started in the seventh year. A new phase began, that of the empty oil drums, from which we tried to construct a subcontinental submarine that could travel freely through the ocean of molten lava under the crust of the earth's surface, from where it could strike without warning and destroy whole cities from underneath, from below their foundations. Ben Hur was appointed captain of the submarine and, as usual, I was his second-in-command, inventor, and chief designer, and responsible for navigation. Chita Reznik, as ordnance officer, collected dozens of yards of old electric wire, together with coils, batteries, switches and insulating tape. Our plan was to sail in our submarine to a point beneath the royal palace in London. Chita had a further, private, objective, which was to use the submarine to capture his two fathers, who spent two or three weeks alternately with his mother, and take them away to a desert island. He loved and respected his mother, and he wanted her to have some peace and quiet because in her youth she had been a famous opera singer in Budapest and now she suffered from attacks of melancholy. (Somebody wrote in red paint on their wall: 'Chita should be very glad – most kids only have one dad. Gladder still is Chita's mother: first she has one then the other.' Chita scratched the writing with a nail, scrubbed it with soap, painted over it, without success.) In Bible class Mr Zerubbabel Gihon taught us about how the Babylonian beasts conquered Jerusalem and our temple and razed them to the ground. As usual he joked at his wife's expense: if Mrs Gihon had lived in Jerusalem in those days the Babylonians would have escaped by the skin of their teeth. He took the opportunity to explain the expression 'skin of their teeth'.

My mother said:

'There's a little girl at the institution, an orphan called Henrietta. Must be five or six. Covered with freckles. She suddenly started calling me her mother, not in Hebrew, in Yiddish, "Mamma", tells everybody I'm her mother, and I can't make up my mind what I ought to do: whether I should tell her I'm not her mother, that her mother's dead – but how can I kill her mother for the second time – or not react, wait for her to get over it. But then what about the other children's jealousy?'

Father said:

'That's difficult. From a moral point of view. Either way someone will suffer. And think of my book: who will read it? They're all dead.'

I didn't find Sergeant Dunlop at the Orient Palace. I looked for him again after the festivals, three times, I still couldn't find him. Not even when the autumn came and low clouds enfolded Jerusalem to remind us that not everything in the world is summer and submarines and underground fighters.

I thought: Maybe he's found out through a complex network of informers and double agents that I was betraying him. That I told Yardena about him and she told her wounded fighter that night, and he told the Underground, and they may have kidnapped him. Or the opposite: maybe the

CID was shadowing us when we met and Sergeant Dunlop has been imprisoned for treason, and maybe because of me he has been removed from his beloved Jerusalem and banished to some far-flung outpost of the Empire, to New Caledonia, New Guinea, or perhaps Uganda or Tanganyika?

What did I have left? Only a little Bible in Hebrew and English that he gave me. I still have it. I couldn't take it to school, because it contained the New Testament, which Mr Gihon said was an anti-Jewish book (but I read it, and I found, among other things, the story of the traitor Judas).

Why didn't I write to Sergeant Dunlop? First of all, he didn't leave me an address. Second, I was afraid that if he got a letter from me it might get him into worse trouble and they might punish him even more. Third, what did I have to say to him?

What about him? Why didn't he write to me? Because he couldn't. After all, I hadn't even told him my name. ('I'm Proffy,' I had said to him, 'a Jew from the Land of Israel.' That's not a sufficient postal address.)

Where in the world are you, Stephen Dunlop, my shy enemy? Wherever you are, in Singapore or Zanzibar, have you found yourself another friend to take my place? Not a friend, a teacher and pupil. Even that is not the right description. What then? What was there between us? To this day I cannot explain to myself what it was. And what do you still remember from the homework I made you do?

I speak as I may.

I have a couple of acquaintances who live in Canterbury. Ten years ago I wrote to them asking them to see if they could find out about him.

Without success.

One of these days I shall pack a small bag and set off for Canterbury myself. I'll hunt through old telephone directories. I'll check in the churches. I'll inquire in the municipal archives. PC 4479. Stephen Dunlop, asthmatic, fond of gossiping, a pink cotton-wool Goliath. A solitary, gentle enemy. A believer in the Prophets. A believer in signs and miracles. If by some miracle, Stephen, this book finds its way into your hands, please drop me a line. Send me a picture postcard, at least. A couple of lines, in Hebrew or English, whichever you prefer.

23

IN SEPTEMBER THERE were more searches. There were imprisonments and a curfew. A lever from a hand grenade was found in Chita's apartment and one of his fathers was taken away for questioning (the other one turned up the same evening). Our teacher Mr Zerubbabel Gihon denounced the Babylonians again in class, and also expressed his doubts as to whether the prophet Jeremiah spoke as befitted a prophet in days of war and siege. In Mr Gihon's view, when the enemy is at the gate, the duty of a prophet is to raise the people's spirits, to unite their ranks, and to pour out his wrath on the foe outside the walls, not on his brethren inside. Above all, a prophet worthy of his name must not insult the royal family and the national heroes. But the prophet Jeremiah was an embittered man and we must try to understand and forgive him.

My mother put up two orphans in our apartment for a few weeks. They were clandestine immigrants and their names were Oleg and Hirsch, but Father declared that henceforth they were to be known as Tzvi and Eyal. We laid the spare mattress out for them on the floor in my bedroom. They were eight or nine years old; even they did not know how old they were, and we mistakenly took them for brothers because they had the same surname, Brinn (which Father Hebraized as Bar-On). But it turned out that they were not brothers, they were not even related; in fact, they were enemies. However, their enmity expressed itself quietly, without violence and almost without words: they knew no Hebrew and it seemed as though they could only talk a little in another language. Despite their hatred of each other, they fell asleep at night on their mattress curled up together like a couple of puppies. I tried to teach them Hebrew and to learn from them something that I could not identify and still cannot explain today, though I knew it was something that those two orphans understood a thousand times better than I did, and better than most grown-ups. After the festivals they were taken away in a pickup truck to a pioneer youth village. Father gave them our old suitcase and my mother packed it with clothes that I had outgrown, asked them to share them without quarrelling, and stroked their heads, which had been shorn for fear of lice. When they were sitting huddled up in the far corner of the truck, Father said to them:

'A new chapter is beginning in your lives.'

And my mother said:

'Come and see us. The spare mattress will always be waiting for you.'

Yes, I told my parents about Yardena. I had to. That is, about the night they went to the commemoration in Tel Aviv and she slept in their room and after midnight a wounded man turned up and Yardena dressed his wounds and before the day dawned he slipped out of the apartment and was gone. I heard it all but saw nothing.

Father said:

'Ho my Kinneret, were you there or was it all just a dream?'

I answered angrily:

'I wasn't dreaming. It really happened. There was an injured man here. I'm sorry I told you about it, because you only make fun of me.'

Mother said:

'The boy's telling the truth.'

And Father:

'Indeed? If that is so, we shall have to have a word with that young lady.'

Mother said:

'It's none of our business.'

And Father:

'But it was definitely a betrayal of trust.'

Mother said:

'Yardena isn't a child any more.'

And Father:

'No, but this child is a child. And in our bed, too, and who knows what sort of vagrant it was? Anyway, we'll talk about this later, just you and I. As for Your Lordship,' he said, 'off to your room with you and get on with your homework.' Which was unfair, because my father knew perfectly well that I always did my homework as soon as I came home from school, first thing, sometimes even before eating the food that was waiting for me in the icebox. But I deserved it because it was unfair of me to tell them about Yardena and the injured man. On the other hand, how could I not tell them? Wasn't I doing my duty? Third. Fourth. Everything I told that I shouldn't have; everything that I should have told but didn't. So I went to my room, and this time, too, I locked the door on the inside and I refused to open it and hardly answered them till the next morning. Even when they knocked on the door. Even when they threatened me with punishment. Even when they were really alarmed (and I was quite sorry for them but I didn't let on). Even when my father said to my mother, on the other side of the door, raising his voice on purpose:

'Never mind. It's not so terrible. It won't hurt him to think things over in the dark.' (He was right about this.)

That evening, alone in my room, hungry but proud and resentful, I thought something like this: Surely there are other secrets in the world apart from liberating the Homeland and the Undergrounds and the British. Hirsch and Oleg, who were taken away in a truck to become pioneers, were they perhaps really brothers who were pretending, for some reason of their own, to be strangers and enemies? Or, on the contrary, were they strangers who sometimes pretended to be brothers? One must observe and keep quiet. Everything has a shadow of some kind. Maybe even a shadow has a shadow.

24

LESS THAN A year after that summer, the English left our Land. The Hebrew State was established. The night it was created it was attacked from every direction by invading Arab armies, but it fought and won and since then it has fought and won over and over again. My mother, who once studied nursing at the Hadassah Hospital, tended the wounded at the first-aid station at the Shibboleth newsstand. At night she was sent to inform the next of kin of those who had been killed, together with the young doctor, Magda Gryphius. In between dealing with the wounded and the dead, she lived at the institution, looking after her orphans. She slept two to three hours a night there on a camp bed in the storeroom. She hardly ever came home. During the war months she took up smoking, and from then on she always smoked, with a bitter expression, as though the cigarettes filled her with disgust. My father continued to compose slogans, but now he also drew up manifestos and leaflets for the fighting units, and he also attended an accelerated course on the use of the mortar. Setting his glasses at a slight angle by raising the arms and thus lowering the lenses a little, he would, responsibly, logically, and correctly dismantle, oil, and reassemble a homemade mortar, screwing each screw sternly, as though he was adding a particularly significant footnote to his book. Ben Hur, Chita, and I filled hundreds of sandbags, helped to dig trenches, and carried messages in a crouching run from one position to another in the days when Jerusalem was besieged and being heavily shelled by the guns of the Kingdom of Transjordan. One shell decapitated an olive tree and the younger of the Sinopsky brothers as he was sitting under the tree with his brother, eating sardines. After the war the elder brother moved to Afula, and the grocery shop was taken over by Chita's two fathers in partnership.

I remember the night at the end of November when the radio announced that in America the United Nations, at a place called Lake Success, had decided to let us set up a Hebrew State, albeit a very small state divided into three blocks. Father came home at one o'clock in the morning from Dr Buster's, where they had all gathered to hear what the radio said about the result of the vote at the UN, and he bent over and stroked my face with his warm hand:

'Wake up. Don't sleep.'

With these words he lifted up my sheet and got into bed next to me fully dressed (he who always insisted so strictly that one must not get into bed in day clothes). He lay in silence for a few minutes, still stroking my face, and I hardly dared to breathe, and all of a sudden he started to talk about things that had never been mentioned in our home before, because it was forbidden, things that I had always known one mustn't ask about and that was that. You couldn't ask him, you couldn't ask my mother, and in general there were a lot of subjects about which the less said the better, and there was an end to it. In a voice of darkness he told me about how it was when he and Mother lived next door to each other as children in a small town in Poland. How the ruffians who lived in the same block abused them, and beat them savagely because the Jews were all rich, idle, and crafty. And how once they stripped him naked in class, at the Gymnasium, by force, in front of the girls, in front of Mother, to make fun of his circumcision. And his own father, Grandpa that is, one of the grandparents that Hitler later murdered, came in a suit and a silk tie to complain to the headmaster but as he was leaving the hoodlums grabbed him and forcibly undressed him, too, in the classroom, in front of the girls. And still in a voice of darkness Father said this to me:

'But from now on there will be a Hebrew State.' And suddenly he hugged me, not gently but almost violently. In the

LIMERICK COUNTY LIBRARY

dark my hand hit his high brow, and instead of his glasses my fingers found his tears. I never saw my father cry, either before that night or since. In fact, I didn't even see him then, only my left hand saw.

WITHDRAWN FROM STOCK

25

SUCH IS OUR story: it comes from darkness, wanders around, and returns to darkness. It leaves behind a memory combining pain and some laughter, regret, wonderment. The paraffin cart went past in the mornings, the paraffin seller sitting on top with the reins hanging slackly in his hands, ringing his handbell and singing a long-drawn-out song in Yiddish to his old horse. The boy who helped at the Sinopsky Brothers grocery had a strange cat that followed him everywhere and wouldn't let him out of its sight. Mr Lazarus, the tailor from Berlin, a nodding, blinking man, shook his head in disbelief: who ever heard of a faithful cat? He said: Perhaps it is a *Geist*, a spirit. The unmarried doctor Magda Gryphius fell in love with an Armenian poet, and followed him to Famagusta in Cyprus. A few years later she returned, bringing with her a flute, and sometimes I would wake up in the night and hear it and a kind of inner whisper said to me, Never forget this, this is the heart of the matter, everything else is only a shadow.

And what is the opposite of what has really happened?

My mother used to say: 'The opposite of what has happened is what has not happened.'

And Father: 'The opposite of what has happened is what is going to happen.'

Once, when we bumped into each other in a little fish restaurant in Tiberias, on the shore of the Sea of Galilee, some fourteen years later, I asked Yardena. Instead of answering me, she burst into her luminous laughter, that laugh that belongs to girls who enjoy being girls and who know pretty well what is possible and what is doomed. Lighting a cigarette, she replied: 'The opposite of what has happened is what might have happened if it weren't for lies and fear.'

These words of hers took me back to the end of that summer, to the sound of her clarinet, to Chita's two fathers, who went on living there after his mother died, to Mr Lazarus, who raised hens on the roof and a few years later decided to remarry, made himself a dark-blue three-piece suit, and invited us all to a vegetarian meal, but that evening, after the wedding and the reception, suddenly jumped off the roof, and to PC 4479, and the panther in the basement, and Ben Hur and the rocket we never sent to London, and also the blue shutter which may still be floating on the stream to this day on its circular journey back to the mill. What is the connection? It is hard to say. And what about the story itself? Have I betrayed them all again by telling the story? Or is it the other way round: would I have betrayed them if I had not told it?

1994–1995

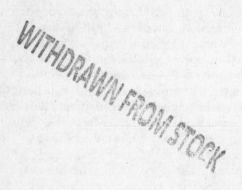

WITHDRAWN FROM STOCK